APPOMATTOX
ROAD

APPOMATTOX ROAD

Final Adventures of the Iron Scouts

MANLY WADE WELLMAN

Ives Washburn, Inc. · *New York*

To *William Lunsford Long and Rosa Heath Long*
neither of whom lacks any characteristic of Southern
gentility or Southern gallantry

Foreword

THOSE who have read the two earlier books about the Iron Scouts know that some of the characters are from history, and that others are real only if imagination can make them so.

In this last story of Iron Scout adventures, maybe some readers will recognize actual happenings during the war between the North and the South. Maybe someone like Clay Buckner played his part in those actual happenings and learned from them to be a good citizen when peace came at last to his country.

—MANLY WADE WELLMAN

Contents

1.	Back to the War	3
2.	Through Enemy Lines	14
3.	A Hundred Circling Camps	26
4.	General Grant's Prisoner	35
5.	Flight and Pursuit	46
6.	The Tricking of Tryon	56
7.	The New Service	65
8.	Richmond	77
9.	Robert E. Lee	89
10.	Fort Stedman	101
11.	"Not Enough of Us"	112
12.	Flight from Petersburg	121
13.	The Terrible March	132
14.	Barricade of Fire	142
15.	Moon over Appomattox	152
16.	Silence	163
17.	The Dawn of Peace	172

APPOMATTOX
ROAD

❧ 1 ❦

Back to the War

Big things seemed to be happening in the little town of Weldon, North Carolina. At its center was a squat railroad depot, from which old red paint had flaked, and around the depot huddled roof-high stacks of freight—bales, packing cases, barrels, chests. Soldiers in shabby Confederate gray stood guard with bright muskets. Most of them were boy-soldiers, with rosy or pale faces on which no beard had yet grown, trying to stand tall and important in rough homespun overcoats too big for them. Officers trudged here and there, checking order blanks against ready shipments, and most of these were grizzled old men or officers who limped from crippling wounds received in action. New Year's noon of 1865 found the Confederate States of America woefully short of fighting men, and Weldon, just below the Virginia line, was a busy dispatch point for troops and supplies for the defenders of besieged Richmond and Petersburg sixty-odd miles northward.

A rusty little engine stood on the tracks opposite the depot, breathing slow, regular puffs of sooty smoke through its funnel-shaped stack. The cars behind it were mostly battered freight cars, just now jammed to overflowing with cargo, but next to the engine were two square-built, dusty-windowed passenger cars. Toward the second of these passenger cars walked lean, young Clay Buckner, gray-uniformed, tawny-haired, and solemn-faced, and Lark Winstead, pretty in dark crinoline and traveling cloak, with a fur-trimmed velvet bonnet on her thick black curls. Clay carried two heavy carpetbags, and under each arm was tucked a big parcel.

"I'm glad my father and mother didn't come to see us off," he said. "It was better just to let Colonel Long's carriage bring us here, without any sad farewells in the depot yard of a strange town."

"I'm just as glad as you are," agreed Lark, her blue eyes thoughtful. "Your parents have treated me like their own daughter all these months I've been staying with them. I was able to say good-by properly there in the parlor, but if they were here now I might cry like a child."

"Child!" repeated Clay, grinning to cheer her up. "Since when did you get so grown up, Miss Lark Winstead?"

"I'm eighteen," she told him severely, "and eighteen is centuries older for a girl than nineteen is for a boy."

"You carry those centuries mighty well," Clay paid her a mock compliment, still smiling. "But don't pull seniority on me—I've been a cavalry scout since a year ago last March." He set down the luggage at the doorstep of the car. "Now then, where did I put our tickets?"

"I have them right here, Scout Buckner. You're too young to trust with important documents."

He was glad that she could joke, too. His two-week holiday furlough, a reward for valuable scouting service in December, had gone too fast. He was trying not to yearn for the home farm in Northampton County, his father and mother and his fifteen-year-old brother, who talked about enlisting in the North Carolina Junior Brigade, the horses and dogs and pigs and chickens. But his furlough was over, and he was due back where they needed him as well as many more like him.

Lark took the tickets from her reticule and handed them to the white-bearded old conductor, who punched them and then helped Clay hoist the carpetbags and parcels up and into the cars. Moving ahead of Clay past a warm black stove, Lark found one of the bench-like wooden seats empty and sat down. Clay stowed the baggage on the shelf above them before he took a seat beside Lark.

"My father says that a man can travel with a pocketful, but a lady has to take along a wagonload," he teased. "And that's the way it's working out with you and me. All I'm taking back is a new uniform and a few things like needles and thread for my friends. You're carrying enough stuff to outfit a regiment—or I'm carrying it for you."

"I'm going to war, too," she reminded him. "I'm going to help Grandfather in Richmond. They've made him chief surgeon of the second largest hospital, and those bags are full of drugs and medicines, right off the blockade runner in Wilmington. And the big square package—"

"That's rations, I know," said Clay, with relish. "You and Mother packed it, and I watched. You put in enough sandwiches and cake and fruit for a dozen."

"It's not a bad idea," Lark insisted.

Her blue eyes searched the car. The other seats were filling up. Near Clay and Lark rode a tired-looking woman with a baby in her arms and two thin little girls. Most of the other passengers were Confederate soldiers. These were gaunt men, most of them bearded and all of them shabby. Like Clay, they were returning to duty after furloughs at home.

A whistle sounded a wheezy warning up ahead, and the car stirred with the grating of wheels beneath. "All aboard!" called the old conductor, and the train began to clank and rattle out of Weldon.

Clay put his broad gray hat in his lap and leaned back. He wondered how the war was going around Petersburg after his two weeks of absence. Vivid in his memory was his adventure when, with others of the audacious Iron Scouts, he had discovered the surprise march of a massive Union column to strike at this very railroad. He had brought the news to the Confederate lines and had pointed the desperate counterstroke that turned back the threat and saved the precious single supply line from the eastern Carolinas to the Army of Northern Virginia in the Petersburg trenches. He had come through the loud peril of battle with only the slightest of flesh wounds in his leg. That, and the gratitude of cavalry commanders, had procured him his furlough home.

Christmas with his family in Northampton County had seemed luxurious after days of perilous riding and spying and nights of bivouac in soggy swamps, but to Clay it had not been a carefree holiday, or even a true relief. For nearly two years his daily duty had been scouting behind and through the menacing lines of blue Federal invaders of the South, at constant risk of capture or death, and he had grown as used to it as a healthy-minded young man in his teens could become. He had a strong sense of responsibility, of the need to return to Sergeant George Shadburne and his other comrades of the Iron Scouts, even now probing shrewdly after the next Union plan of attack.

Lark Winstead, the Virginia girl who had been visiting his parents, seemed to feel something of that same uneasy sense of duty. Lark was going to Richmond, the surrounded, half-starved capital of the Confederacy, to do what she could to assist her grandfather. Dr. Winstead was an overworked but resolute old man in the hospital service, and he trusted Lark, depended on her. Clay had been trying to tease, but he heartily approved of his companion. He had known Lark since first he had come to the war in Virginia. He had seen her work hard, intelligently, and sometimes dangerously. The two of them had served as a team of spy-hunters in Richmond the previous spring, had won the

praise of President Davis and General Custis Lee. Lark
Winstead was as brave as the bravest, Clay knew—as
brave as the Iron Scouts themselves.

They rolled over mildly wintry landscape. Cows
and horses cropped dry yellow grass; cabin chimneys
smoked. Under their seat, the car wheels clanked and
rattled decrepitly. Up in the front of the car, two
ragged soldiers lifted their voices in song, tenor and
baritone:

"On the plains of Manassas the Yankees we met,
 And we gave them a whipping they'll never forget,
 But I ain't got no money, nor nothing to eat—
 I'm afraid that tonight I must sleep in the street."

Applause rang through the car from front to back.
"More! More!" bawled other passengers, and the
singers obliged:

"Your parents despise me, they think I'm too poor,
 They think I'm unworthy to enter your door—"

Half a dozen more gray clad soldiers joined in,
Clay Buckner among them:

"Oh Molly, dear Molly, you've caused me to roam,
 I'm a poor rebel soldier and Dixie's my home."

The mock-tragic verses brought an atmosphere of
friendly good feeling aboard, and the passengers began
to chatter, ask each other's name, and exchange gossip.

"Are you getting hungry?" Lark asked Clay after an
hour had passed.

" Lark, I'm always getting hungry. Shall I fetch down those commissary stores up above us?"

"Get both packages."

He rose and did so. Lark opened the bigger of the two, and Clay, standing beside the seat, whistled his admiration.

"I didn't think there could be that many sandwiches in the whole Confederacy," he vowed.

"All right, now help me. Pick up that bale of food and follow me down the aisle."

Lark got up and moved ahead of him, passing out sandwiches to the hungry soldiers. Their eyes gleamed gratefully above their beards.

"Thank you, miss."

"God bless you, young lady—this is like home, only more so."

"I do thank you, and that's a fact."

Happily they gobbled sandwiches. When the first package was emptied, Clay fetched the second, and Lark led him into the next car to distribute food to soldiers there. They returned to their own seat with what was left.

"Won't you have something?" Lark asked the tired mother across the aisle from them.

The woman looked at the food with honest longing, but shook her head. "Don't want to take your dinner," she protested.

"Oh, we have enough," Lark assured her. "Here, take sandwiches for the little girls, and these apples."

Clay carried the wrappings of the packages to the

stove, opened the door and stuffed them in. Returning, he found Lark unfolding a white napkin.

"We still have two big sandwiches," she said, smiling. "It wasn't really too many, was it?"

"Just enough," he told her, biting into bread and home-smoked ham.

The train moved along with steady determination, but not with any great speed. They might be averaging twelve or fourteen miles an hour, Clay figured as he munched. Up through Virginia they smoked and trundled their way. Once, far away to the right, rose a sound as of many drums rolling. Every soldier in the car sat up and peered through his window. It was artillery fire.

"I'd half forgotten how that sounded," said Lark.

"You'll get used to it right quickly, back in Richmond," Clay assured her. "It's louder and meaner around Petersburg. Of course, I won't be in Petersburg much—I'll hit for Blackwater Swamp and the Iron Scouts again."

"You'll be mighty careful, Clay," pleaded Lark.

He laughed and shook his tawny head. "I'm not going to have time to be careful. Not and do my scouting. When this war's all over, Lark, then maybe I'll have the time to sit down and be scared and worried over what might have happened to me."

"When this war's all over," she repeated, almost inaudibly. She was not laughing with him this time. "When will that be?"

He shook his head again. "I don't know. I doubt if anybody knows—President Davis or General Lee, Lincoln or Grant, or George Shadburne or anybody. All I can say is, I want to be around to feel glad when the day comes."

"When the Confederate States of America are free and victorious," she summed up, so grimly that Clay glanced at her sidelong.

"I do admire you lady-folks," he confessed. "In the army, we don't talk about whether we'll win or lose the war. We just hope we'll win, and that we'll live to see it. But you and my mother and your grandmother and all the other ladies don't think of anything but victory."

"We dare not think of anything but victory," she told him.

"Just keep thinking about it," he said, his smile gone too. "Maybe that's what we need to help us get it."

Midafternoon came, and shadows began to lengthen. The train rumbled over a rickety railroad bridge that crossed a clammy-looking creek. On the far side riders in gray appeared from among leafless thickets to canter beside the cars. The locomotive blew its whistle and the Confederate cavalry responded with shrill Rebel yells of welcome.

"We're getting to the cavalry camp," said Clay. "That's where I drop off."

The train slowed down in a broad open space set with tents and huts and makeshift shelters of poles and boards and bundled dry grass. Lines of picketed horses stood at either side of the tracks. The locomotive put on its decrepit brakes with a great squeaking crash, and Clay rose from his seat.

"Good-by, Lark," he said. "I'll try to get up to Richmond to see you one of these days."

"I'll walk out with you," she told him.

But as Clay swung down the steps onto trampled earth, a white-haired old man in a shabby gray officer's coat limped forward, cane in hand.

"I came down from Richmond to ride back with Lark," said Dr. Winstead. "Clay, my boy, it's good to see you looking so healthy. I don't have a great deal to do with healthy folks these days."

"Grandfather!" cried Lark, and ran past Clay to hug the doctor in happy welcome. Then she turned to Clay, put her hands on his shoulders, and kissed him quickly.

"Good-by, Clay," she said in his ear, "and be careful. Even if you don't have time to—be careful, please."

"I'll do my best, Lark," he promised, and she and her grandfather mounted the car steps.

The train crawled away. Lark stood on the platform waving her hand, and Dr. Winstead lifted his broad hat. Clay watched until he could see them no more, then tramped away toward the cluster of tents where cavalry headquarters were maintained.

The headquarters guard detail was from the First North Carolina Cavalry, Clay's regiment in the days before he was transferred to the scouting service. Shouts of recognition arose.

"Clay Buckner's back from home, boys!"

"Let's rub some mud on that pretty new uniform he's brought back!"

"We heard you was goin' to be colonel of one of them new Junior Reserve regiments, Clay!"

"That ain't so; Clay's too old to be a Junior Reserve colonel!"

Through the knot of grinning troopers slid a brown-bearded man in a blue forage cap and a seedy gray cavalry cape, moving with casual assurance.

"Got your letter, Clay," said Sergeant George Shadburne, "so I thought I'd slip through the Yankee lines to meet you."

"Sergeant George!" cried Clay, and shook hands joyfully. "Where's our camp?"

"Same place as it was when you left." That meant the depths of Blackwater Swamp; Shadburne would not name the spot, not even among these cavalrymen of his own army.

"Are the boys all right?"

"Some of them are, and some are—" Shadburne's mouth went grim in its mask of beard. "Some are gone. I'm glad we've got you back, because there's plenty to do. Let's get ready to sneak back past the Yankees and go home."

≈ 2 ≈

Through Enemy Lines

Sergeant George Shadburne and Private Clay Buckner trudged away from the cavalry lines. On the far side of the camp they plunged into soggy, leafless woods, followed a half-hidden trail northeast, and came to a slow, chill stream with a tumble-down log house on the far side.

Here on the bank where they paused waited half a dozen troopers on picket. The corporal in charge barked out a challenge; but then he immediately recognized Shadburne, shook his hand, and offered two of the picket party's horses to carry the scouts across the ford dry-shod.

"Just turn them nags loose on the other side," the corporal called. "They'll head back to us when we whistle for them."

On the shore beyond, Clay and Shadburne dismounted. When the corporal emitted a shrill whistle, the two horses splashed obediently back.

"They're smart enough for Iron Scout horses," commented Shadburne. "Let's head north here; we aren't far from our bivouac."

In among more dripping trees they walked.

"You said we lost some of the Iron Scouts," said Clay.

"That's right. We lost Shake Harris and Wallace Miller and Sol Legare." Shadburne spoke the names unhappily. "They were captured while you were gone. I haven't heard anything about Miller or Legare, but Shake's in the Yankee war prison at Point Lookout in Maryland, double-shackled and double-guarded, swearing he'll escape in spite of General Grant himself."

"How about Jim Sloan?" asked Clay. "And Bob Dulin?"

"Sloan will be in camp yonder, mighty happy to shake the hand of his fellow Tarheel. Bob's still counting up how many more Yankees he has to bring down to make up that hundred he wants before the war's over."

"Bob's never forgiven the deaths of his brothers," said Clay.

"No, he hasn't," Shadburne agreed, and shook his head moodily. "I reckon thousands of folks's brothers have been disposed of already. I wish sometimes that Bob would tell himself that nothing will bring those brothers of his back again. Now take it slow and quiet here, Clay; I think there's a blue-coated picket up ahead."

They crouched doubled over as they slid together through dense brush. Practiced at penetrating such cover, neither of them rustled a dry twig or shook a branch. Then Shadburne dropped to his hands and knees and crept forward as swiftly and surely as a lizard. Clay crawled after him. At last Shadburne stopped and motioned for a halt. He turned around.

"Look," his bearded lips mouthed silently, and he pointed ahead.

Clay lifted himself cautiously on his hands to peer through a crisscross of branches. He saw that they were on the edge of a field once cleared of timber but now overgrown with scrubby trees and dried weeds. Among the taller trees at the far side rose a slender plume of smoke from a campfire.

"Yankees on picket," whispered Shadburne softly. "That's their headquarters' fire."

Clay glanced to right and left. More trees enclosed the field on either hand. "They'll probably have plenty of observers out to both sides," he ventured in an undertone.

"Right," agreed Shadburne, with a quick nod of his blue-capped head. "And they won't be expecting any advance straight across this field. So that's what we'll do: head directly at them."

He flung himself down again and wormed out from the thicket in among the weeds and scrub. Clay followed him, almost flat on the damp, half-frozen ground. The winter-killed growth of grassy weeds was just tall enough to conceal their slow-moving bodies in a prone position, but not an inch taller.

It seemed to take an hour of laborious creeping to cross that shaggy expanse, with rests here and there where the cover was thickest and highest. Clay found himself sweating despite the chill that was growing in the late afternoon. At last they reached the trees on the opposite edge. Under the nearest low branches they sat up on their heels, stretching their necks and straining their ears.

Fire flickered brightly just ahead. Clay smelt pungent smoke from the burning wood. Again Shadburne led the way on all fours, bearing to the right of the fire. The floor of the forest was slimy with wet. The knees of Clay's new uniform soaked through clammily, and his hands were splashed to the wrists. Taking advantage of every stump, hummock, and half-rotten log, they worked their way past the fire, so near to it that they could hear voices in conversation. Then Shadburne came to a stop again, and beckoned Clay to squirm forward to a position beside him.

They had passed through a wide belt of trees and had come to the edge of another and larger field. Perhaps fifty or sixty yards ahead of them they saw a line of breastworks made of earth heaped massively over felled logs. On the other side the pointed tops of tents appeared. Blue-uniformed sentinels with muskets on their shoulders paced behind the entrenchments, their capped heads visible.

"A big fortified camp," Clay half-groaned.

"Keep your voice down, Clay," muttered Shadburne. "I knew this camp was here; I've figured what we'll do. Here, hold this."

He flung off the gray cape and revealed himself in

blue cavalry jacket and breeches, with knee boots and pistol belt. On his shoulders were the barred straps of a Federal captain. He drew the big revolver from its holster at his side.

"You haven't got any weapons, have you?" he whispered. "No? Good. Just follow whatever cues I give you. Stand up and carry that cape."

Clay rose, wondering. At once Shadburne raised his voice.

"Halt, you Rebel spy!" he thundered furiously. "Make one false move and I'll fire!"

He jerked his head for Clay to follow him into the open. "You're my prisoner!" he roared at the top of his lungs.

"What's that?" came a shout from the trees through which they had just crept. There was a crashing, hurried movement. A Union soldier sprang into view, musket at the ready. After him rushed another soldier, and then a big sergeant with three stripes on his thick arm.

"What's happening here?" demanded the sergeant.

"That's just what I'm trying to find out," growled Shadburne. Then, glaring at Clay: "You nearly sneaked into our lines, didn't you? Well, I'm going to see that you get a whole lot deeper in than you figured on—right into prison, Johnny Reb!"

"We'll take charge of him for you, Captain," offered the sergeant briskly, and Clay felt apprehensive, but Shadburne gestured the suggestion away with the barrel of his revolver.

"Wait a minute, Sergeant. This Rebel has a mighty big bunch of uniform for one of Lee's ragged band. He's wearing an overcoat and carrying a fine gray cape. You've got a partner in this business, Johnny. Tell us where he is."

"I refuse to answer," replied Clay, with a fine show of sullen defiance.

"Give me that," the sergeant ordered, and snatched Shadburne's cape from over Clay's arm. He explored the big pocket in the lining and brought a handful of papers into view.

"Let me look at those," Shadburne commanded. "Keep this man covered, you others. He's not to escape."

He took the papers from the sergeant and riffled through them, making a show of stern examination.

"I see the name of Shadburne here," he announced gruffly. "Is that Sergeant George Shadburne, the Iron Scout?"

"I've heard of him, sir," spoke up one of the soldiers.

"We've all heard of him," added the sergeant.

"Speak up," Shadburne commanded Clay. "Is your Sergeant Shadburne sneaking around here?"

"He might be closer to you than you think, right now," replied Clay enigmatically.

"Where?" the sergeant snapped. "Where is Shadburne?"

"Suppose you find out," Clay said, folding his arms with dignity. "That's what you're on picket for."

"These men will find him," Shadburne said. "Sergeant, let your party comb these woods thoroughly. If any Iron Scouts are prowling, capture them. And if they resist, then—"

He flourished his revolver significantly.

"We understand, sir," replied the sergeant, saluting. "All right, boys! Get the rest of the reserve here, and spread out and shake these woods down from top to bottom!"

"And this prisoner goes to headquarters for questioning," wound up Shadburne. "Come along with me, Rebel, but don't make a false move if you have the least regard for your health."

He waved Clay toward the breastworks with his big revolver. A score of blue infantry were gazing above the parapet at them, with a row of muskets to the fore, but Shadburne herded Clay close to them with all the assurance in the world.

"Everybody on the alert!" Shadburne yelled harshly at the waiting faces. "Those woods have Iron Scouts in them!"

"Iron Scouts!" a young soldier echoed eagerly. "Show me one!"

"This prisoner is one, but leave him to me."

Shadburne waved grandly for Clay to climb over the earthwork, then scrambled over after him and dropped down on the other side among watching bluecoats.

"Who's in command here?" asked Shadburne. "You, Lieutenant? Well, be ready to support those pickets if they're driven in. I'll take this man to headquarters and see if we can't make him talk about what the Rebels are up to."

Confidently he marched Clay away toward the rear. The men at the rampart took no notice of them; all their attention was directed toward the woods. Shadburne and Clay threaded their way between two expanses of tents. Beyond stood a row of larger tents, the sort used by officers in the Federal army. Into one of these Shadburne walked as though he owned it. Clay followed him.

"Nobody at home to greet us," said Shadburne, "but there hangs a fine blue overcoat that might fit you. That sergeant went off with my cape, so you take that one. It's big enough to cover your overcoat nicely."

Clay pulled on the big coat and turned up its wide collar, then belted a shining saber outside it. He thrust his Confederate slouch hat inside the bosom of the coat and appropriated a blue forage cap like Shadburne's. They emerged, very much the picture of a pair of Northern officers on tour. Beyond the tents they found lines of tethered horses, with here and there a trooper grooming his mount. Near at hand a dapper orderly held the bridles of four fine animals.

"We'll take these two," said Shadburne authoritatively, walking up and pointing.

The orderly saluted, but stared his lack of comprehension.

"There's some mistake, Captain," he ventured.

"Mistake? What do you mean, orderly? Whose horses are these?"

"They belong to Colonel Holtzburger and his aides, sir."

"Colonel Holtzburger, eh?" echoed Shadburne. "Then there's no mistake; he told me to help myself. Here, give the colonel this when he comes back."

From inside his blouse he whipped a notebook and pencil, scribbled impressively, tore out the page and thrust it into the orderly's hands. Then he and Clay mounted the two best-looking horses and rode away to the eastward. They passed more and larger camps, but were not challenged.

"That's how to get back and forth to our positions, my friend," grinned Shadburne at last. "Act as if you own everything everywhere, North or South. All right, we're out of sight of them now. Follow me."

He shook his bridle. His horse galloped away. Clay hurried his own stolen mount at Shadburne's heels.

Their road lay between thick-growing, swampy trees. Shadburne reined to the right and into a narrow woodland trail that would take a sharp eye to find. Clay kept after him while they splashed through dank marshy mud and among dark brooding cypresses. A rotting rail fence barred their way, but Shadburne put his horse to the jump and soared over, Clay after him. Beyond was a brook to wade across, then more trees, thickly matted with vines under which both riders had to stoop as they rode to keep from being dragged out of the saddle.

Finally they emerged upon the bank of a river. Evening was descending upon them, dull gray and cold.

"I know where we are now," spoke up Clay. "This is the Blackwater."

"High time you recognized your own front yard. Let's tell the boys we're coming in."

Pursing his lips, Shadburne gave vent to a long, quavering cry like that of an owl. A moment of silence, then it was answered from across the river. Another moment, and the call was repeated.

"That means it's all clear," pronounced Shadburne. "Let's go."

He kicked his mount's sides to force it into the water. The slow, cold current surged to the very saddle girths, wetting the riders' booted feet, but the horses came safely across the ford and up the bank on the other side. As they entered a new density of woods, a laugh sounded at Clay's elbow and a rider appeared.

"Welcome home, prodigal," said a merry voice he recognized. "Too bad we don't have a fatted calf already barbecued for you."

Happily Clay reached out his hand to greet young Hugh Scott. Up ahead another familiar form rode into sight. It was Jim Sloan. The four of them walked their horses through a screen of vine-tangled, moisture-beaded pine, and then they were in camp.

Half a dozen huts made of boughs and plastered over with mud huddled close around a central space with a fire burning and a piece of ragged tent canvas rigged overhead. As Shadburne and Clay dismounted, the Iron Scouts came out of the huts and clustered around to ask questions.

"What's it like between here and Petersburg?" demanded Scott.

"They've flung up new breastworks right across our way, but Clay and I slid through them like an eel," replied Shadburne. "I don't know whether the same trick will work twice, so we'll scout out a place where the Yankees haven't made themselves quite as much to home."

"How did you leave the folks in North Carolina?" Sloan asked Clay. "How's that pretty girl Lark Winstead?"

"She came back to Richmond to her grandfather," Clay informed him. "She's going to help him at the hospital."

"One more reason for you to get yourself wounded," chuckled Barney Hennegan, the huge giant of the Iron Scouts.

Clay and Shadburne unsaddled their captured horses and tethered them with the line of fine chargers the Iron Scouts kept. A happy whinny greeted Clay, and he stopped to pat his own favorite mount, sleek brown Cherokee, who had carried him at Chancellorsville, in the Wilderness, going after the Federal raiders who had attempted to strike the railroad. They all returned to the fireside, where a huge skillet of fish was frying for supper. Bill Mikler was acting as cook, and with justifiable pride he heaped tin plates with johnnycakes and sweet potatoes roasted in the ashes to supplement the fish. Clay sat down between

Hugh Scott and another youngster of his own age, dark, moody Bob Dulin.

"What do your home folks say about the war?" asked Bob, chewing fish.

"What they've always said," replied Clay. "That they want the war to go on until the South has won."

"That might be quite some time yet," observed Scott, reaching out a big tin cup for coffee from Bill Mikler's pot.

"It had better be a long time," growled Bob Dulin. "I haven't got my hundred Yanks yet."

"Oh, come now," called Shadburne from the other side of the fire. "Are you set on that score of a hundred again?"

"Again?" echoed Bob. "I never was any other way but set on it, and I'm going to make it before the fighting's over."

≽ 3 ≼

A Hundred Circling Camps

The Iron Scouts lived like otters in the depths of Blackwater Swamp, far from their own army and with the Union besiegers cutting them off from their commanders; but they made themselves comfortable between their tours of duty. Their permanent headquarters were the little cluster of low-built huts in the thickest tangle of the swamp, with cunningly woven screens of branches and vines to hide their fires. The approach to their haven was through the deepest and most watery mud in all the region, and they alone knew the winding, treacherous trails. As for supplies, they had long depended on their Northern adversaries for those.

Inside the huts on improvised bunks of poles and pine-needle mattresses were spread blankets of Union army issue. Camp chests were ammunition boxes snatched from unwary Federal artillery positions. Hanging on the mud-plastered walls of the huts were spare clothing—coats, breeches, and hats of blue Union cloth, the plunder of many a foray. Weapons were of

Union make, too—revolvers and carbines and sabers. And the food the Iron Scouts ate was in large part from Union army stores, stolen under the noses of regimental and brigade commissaries who did not dream a Southern forager would venture near.

Helping to wash the tin plates and cups after supper, Clay listened to his friends as they sang their own favorite song:

"We're scouts for the Rebel army,
   Our fame goes far and wide—
When the Yankees hear us coming,
   They fling down their guns and hide. . . ."

But they sang softly, Clay thought; they sang almost plaintively.The Iron Scouts had not lost their determination and daring and skill, but some of the gaiety was gone. Quite a few of the Scouts were gone, too. Shadburne, their peerless leader, had far fewer men now to come at his call than in the joyous days of triumph before Chancellorsville and Gettysburg. Yet some of the best still survived, perhaps, because they were of the best. Young Hugh Scott, beside Clay, scrubbed plates with sand. Yonder by the fire lounged Barney Hennegan, huge rock of a man who was able to bend iron horseshoes with his broad paws. Bill Mikler was there, too, and beard-tufted Jack Shoolbred, and Jim Sloan who like Clay had come from North Carolina. And at the door of a hut squatted the dark, moody Bob Dulin, painstakingly pulling his revolver to pieces and oiling it though it seemed immaculate, while dreaming his bitter dream of killing a hundred Union soldiers. In another camp in the swamp, Shadburne had told Clay, Dick Hogan commanded more Iron Scouts, observing toward the main headquarters of the Army of the Potomac at City Point.

Clay racked up the plates and washed his own hands in a battered iron basin, just as Shadburne strolled close in the firelit night.

"Ready to take a ride tomorrow?" he asked.

"Why not?" Clay returned. "I've had a good rest at home; it's time I did some work to earn my twelve Confederate dollars a month."

"That's what I was thinking. Sit down and stir up the fire so we can see these papers. I did all right, keeping them from being carried off in my cloak by that Yankee picket sergeant, didn't I? What we're supposed to do is map out the whole line of forts and strong points around our own Petersburg trenches."

He handed Clay a roughly penciled chart. Sitting cross-legged, Clay studied it carefully. "This seems to be mapped out pretty well already, Sergeant."

"It's the last map I drew. They're changing all the time—that breastwork you and I tricked our way over today is a brand-new one within the last few days. The Yankees keep straightening out a crook in the line here, building up a new position there, taking troops from one point and concentrating them at another. It's up to us to figure all these things out and get the news through to Marse Robert Lee, so that he can guess where their next poke at his defenses is going to take place."

"Let me copy this so I can puzzle out all the changes," said Clay.

"Yes, do that. You're one of the best mapmakers in the whole bunch. I think I'll put you with Mikler and Scott, and give each of you a segment of the Yankee line to spy out. I suppose you'll want to ride that Cherokee horse of yours."

"Cherokee's getting sort of well-known among the Federal cavalry," Clay said. "If I ride him into their lines, somebody might recognize him. Why don't I use that horse I picked up today?"

"No reason why you shouldn't. Go ahead."

There were days of scouting and mapmaking duty for Clay. Shadburne assigned him the task of reconnoitering the right of the Federal line of works, from the Appomattox River east of Petersburg down to the head of the Blackwater. Clay rode in blue Federal uniform on the horse captured behind the breastworks, and Shadburne had provided him with a forged paper identifying him as Private John Pollock, a courier from Union headquarters at City Point.

For many months it had been Clay's regular duty to ride and spy among Federal armies, but once again he was almost bewildered by the numbers of the blue-coats. Huge concentrations of troops lay in tented camps around Petersburg. He saw where whole sections of timberland had been chopped away to make firewood for the vast armies of Ulysses S. Grant. Regiment after regiment of well-equipped, smartly disciplined, battle-seasoned troops ringed the beleaguered Confederates, with massive fortifications to the front. He contrived to visit these fortifications, riding confidently under pretense of delivering orders and reports to commanding officers. Secretly he noted down all that he saw.

The strong point nearest the Blackwater River was called Fort Rice, and here was hollowed out an elaborate system of defenses and bombproof shelters, with thick banks of earth facing toward Petersburg and heavy guns mounted at strategic points. A trench with a parapet connected Fort Rice with a similar sturdy redoubt called Fort Meikle, and beyond Fort Meikle was Fort Horton, set on high ground that would be difficult to storm from the Petersburg side. And next to Fort Haskell, at a quarter-mile's distance, was Fort Stedman.

This position, as Clay found out from a visit, was much the strongest in his whole area of investigation. It included several rows of deep-spaded ditches, their sides stoutly faced with poles and roughly split planks; and frowning massively toward the Confederate lines was a strong sloping breastwork of earth tamped down over big logs.

Behind and near Fort Stedman no less than six batteries of big guns were massed, and in the trenches there and to either side stood infantry, sent forward from the reserve camps in the rear of the main line.

Beyond the breastwork, in the woods and old fields between the two armies, strong pickets lurked on duty day and night.

To the east of Fort Stedman were nearly three-quarters of a mile of trenches, backed up by more guns. The final strong point was Fort McGilvrey, on the shore of the Appomattox east of the Petersburg defenses.

Clay moved here and there with a show of the utmost assurance, as though he were a part of it all. He was accepted by the Union troops as one of themselves, and again and again he sat down with a squad off duty to share a meal of hardtack and salt pork and drink strong black coffee. He even joined in their singing, learning different songs from those that were popular with the Army of Northern Virginia. One in particular impressed him:

"I have seen Him in the watchfires of a hundred circling camps. . . ."

That was the "Battle Hymn of the Republic," sung to the tune of "John Brown's Body." And these were the hundred circling camps, Clay felt, their watchfires thronged with stalwart, brave fighting men, ready to battle it out to the last drop of blood and the last charge of powder. Facing these myriads, as Clay knew, were Lee's shrunken regiments, forces so reduced that every unit was on duty in the trenches nearly all the time. Clay had heard that one man of every three must stand with musket ready behind the banks of earth, while a second was ready to join him in case of attack, and only the third of the three could relax in the trench eating, sleeping, or wondering how it was going to end.

A full week Clay spent in completing his careful survey of the forts and trenches between the Appomattox and the Blackwater. He returned to the headquarters of the Iron Scouts and gave his notes and sketches to Shadburne, who studied them soberly.

"You've done right well, Clay," approved the sergeant at last. "Not only the locations and descriptions of each fort, but what regiments are camped along the line, with the names of their commanding officers." He tapped Clay's rough map with his finger. "The one that looks most important is Fort Stedman," he decided. "They've been improving and strengthening their position there, and concentrating artillery."

"Our own guns are especially strong opposite," said Clay.

"Nowhere as strong as these numbers. They may be planning a bombardment and an assault at that point. Go back and see what preparations are being made— rations, supplies of ammunition, and so on. I'll wait here for your report."

Again Clay rode forth, on an evening as gray and cold as those inadequate defense lines around Petersburg. He knew all the trails from the Blackwater to the Appomattox by now, and chose approaches where there was the least chance of meeting Federal patrols.

By dusk he was close to the camps behind Fort Rice. Then he reined in and jumped down from his saddle. He had heard motion among the trees ahead of him.

His horse emitted a soft, friendly, nickering sound —other horses were coming that way. At once Clay clamped a hand over the horse's nose and caught the rein close to the bit, leading the animal in between two broad tree trunks. Stifling the horse's efforts to voice a neighed greeting, he listened.

Heavy hoofs fell. A voice spoke, another replied. Then he spotted two men, on foot and leading their horses. The dying light of day showed that they wore gray uniforms. They were heading straight for the Federal camp just beyond the trees.

"Be careful!" called Clay, louder than he meant to.

At once both men stopped. The tallest whipped out a revolver.

"Stand easy, boys, I'm a friend." Clay came into view from between the trees, leading his own mount with him. "You'd better turn back. There's a whole campful of Yankees—regiments of them—up ahead there."

"Is that so?" inquired the tall man with the drawn revolver. "But you're a Yankee, judging by those clothes."

"Not me," Clay assured him. "I'm blue outside, but I'm pure Rebel inside."

"Then," said the tall man, "suppose you hold up your hands."

Clay stared at him. "Why, what—"

"Hands up," rasped the other of the two grayjackets. He had a revolver, too, and he pointed it straight into Clay's face. "You're our prisoner."

Clay let go of the bit strap and lifted his hands into the air.

"You don't understand," he argued. "This is a Federal uniform, all right, but—"

"But you say there's a Rebel inside it," finished the tall man for him. "And we wear Rebel uniforms, but inside them we're Union. Now do you see what's happened to you?"

Clay looked so blank that his two captors burst out laughing at him.

"We're Jessie Scouts," the tall one told him. "Combing these woods for spies like you. I take it that you're a scout yourself—maybe an Iron Scout."

"Take it whatever way you like, sir," said Clay tonelessly. "I'll tell you nothing."

The shorter man heaved a deep sigh. "That means he's an Iron Scout, all right. And orders say to bring any Iron Scouts we find straight to General Grant himself at City Point."

≫ 4 ≪

General Grant's Prisoner

While the tall Federal in gray kept Clay at pistol point, the smaller one, a squat, sorrel-haired man of thirty, came to him, snatched the revolver from his belt and the saber from his saddle, and dived into his pockets. He brought out the false paper identifying Clay as Private John Pollock.

"This settles it," he assured Clay grimly. "I happen to know the headquarters' couriers at City Point, and there's not any John Pollock among them. What's your real name, Iron Scout—George Shadburne?"

"Just call me Stonewall Jackson," said Clay.

"Come on, tell us your name," coaxed the taller man. He had black hair and high cheekbones. "We know your whole Iron Scout bunch. Are you Hugh Scott? Bill Mikler? Dick Hogan?"

"I never heard of any of them," Clay replied. "Introduce me some time."

"Well, we've put Shake Harris and Sol Legare and Wallace Miller in prison," offered the other Jessie Scout. "You can shake hands with them when you go there and the door clanks shut behind you."

They allowed him to mount, but the short man kept the reins of his horse, and both held their weapons ready as they rode toward the camp with Clay between them. Sentries challenged the gray uniforms excitedly, but the Jessie Scouts gave the countersign and passed in to report to the officer of the day.

Someone recognized the horse Clay rode as belonging to Colonel Holtzburger. Clay was put in the stockade behind the guardhouse, with chains at his wrists and ankles, and the guards were alerted to special attention. Supper was brought him—a good supper, steaming hot beans and bacon, hardtack, and strong coffee—and he slept on Union army blankets spread on the ground.

At dawn the next day he was wakened to eat sowbelly and drink more coffee, and his captors of the previous evening appeared, their gray jackets changed for blue. They led Clay out and showed him a sleepy-eyed, droopy-eared brown mule with a wreck of a saddle strapped to its back.

"Mount that, my boy," invited the tall Jessie Scout. "I doubt if you're going to break away and gallop back to your camp on him. He won't buck and he won't race, but he'll cover ground, and that's what we're to cover today."

After a hasty breakfast, they began a long ride between strong fortifications to the left hand and encamped reserves on the right, then a journey along the south bank of the Appomattox. Clay's guards chatted with him like old acquaintances. They told him their names—the tall man was Dave Wagner and his sorrel-haired partner was Ike Murray. The Jessie Scouts, they said, had been organized by General Sheridan and named for Mrs. Jessie Frémont, wife of the picturesque Federal general who once had explored California and had run for president.

"We do what you Iron Scouts do," said Ike Murray. "We filter through your lines and snap up little pieces of news that might entertain General Grant and his staff."

"We learned some tricks from Mosby's Rangers," added Dave Wagner, "and a few extra frills lately from Shadburne and your other friends. Come on, sonny, what's your real name?"

"Nathan Bedford Forrest," said Clay. "I've just been transferred from the West to clean you Yankees up."

"You look more like Jeff Davis to me," offered Murray, studying Clay with a great show of canny shrewdness.

"How did you ever guess it?" Clay asked him, and all three of them laughed.

At noon, Murray and Wagner reined in, dug into their saddlebags, and produced crackers and cheese and a tin of sardines. These good things they shared with Clay. The ride along the Appomattox continued in an almost friendly spirit, except that Clay stubbornly refused to admit that he had any connection with, or knowledge of, the Iron Scouts.

They came at last to where a pontoon bridge, closely

and heavily guarded, spanned the river. They rode over it and beyond until early sunset, when the guard below City Point challenged them.

Clay was acquainted with City Point from other visits. It was mostly a string of wharfs thronged with Federal supply steamers, a knot of wooden buildings on a river shore, and clusters of tents. Dismounting, the three walked toward the largest building. From the flagpole on top of it, a noncommissioned officer was pulling down the Stars and Stripes for the night.

A sentry on the shabby porch slanted his musket across his chest to bar their way and ask their business.

"Scouts with an important prisoner," Dave Wagner informed him. "General Grant wants to see this man."

"Who is he?" asked the sentry.

"He's owned up to being Stonewall Jackson, Bedford Forrest, and Jeff Davis," replied Ike Murray. "Does that sound important enough to get us past you?"

"Corporal!" bawled the sentry, and a small, spectacled man with a double stripe on his right arm stuck his head out the door.

"Hello, Wagner," the corporal said. "Who's that you're bringing with you?"

"He won't admit it, but we think he's one of the Iron Scouts."

"An Iron Scout, huh? Bring him inside."

Clay marched in ahead of his two captors. He found himself in a large room set with desks at which noncommissioned officers were busy with papers. Along one wall extended a bench on which lounged a row of soldiers, each with a musket across his knees. The corporal knocked at one of several doors at the rear of the room, entered, and spoke to someone inside. Then he reappeared.

"Fetch in that prisoner."

Clay crossed the floor and entered the open doorway. Inside, a blue-uniformed officer with close-clipped brown side whiskers glanced up from his desk, then fairly jumped to his feet, smiling as though in happy welcome.

"Welcome to my office, Clay Buckner!" he cried.

"Tryon!" cried Clay.

He knew this Yankee officer, had fought against him, and learned to respect and like him. "It's Colonel Tryon now, isn't it?" Clay asked.

"That's right." Tryon shook hands cordially with Clay. "I'm on General Grant's staff now, clear out of the spy business, as you know." He nodded to the amazed Wagner and Murray. "It's all right, men. You can relax, unless Mr. Buckner here tries to fly out of the window. He and I know each other well. We've tried to outguess and outrun each other in Northern Virginia and Richmond and practically everywhere. Sit down, Clay, and tell me the news."

Sitting down himself, Colonel Tryon smiled expectantly at his prisoner.

"Sir," said Wagner respectfully, "do you identify this man as an Iron Scout?"

"Certainly I do," said Tryon. "I've been a prisoner of the Iron Scouts, and I know them well. Splendid fellows, every one of them, good shots and good riders and good soldiers—and as full of poison against the Union as a Richmond drugstore. But," and he smiled again, "Clay Buckner and I are like special old comrades. In fact, once the Union was going to hang him and the Confederates were going to hang me. Then they traded us, one for the other. That's why we both feel grateful. Right, Clay?"

"Right, Colonel," said Clay honestly.

"Sir," said Wagner again, "we understood that General Grant would want to question any Iron Scout we might bring in."

Tryon laughed aloud. "Oh, yes. You two want it put on your records that you made this important capture. I'll see to that. How did you bag him?"

Wagner told the story. Again Tryon whooped with laughter, slapping his neat-trousered thigh.

"Clay," he said, "you must be getting old and war-worn to blunder into a trap like that. Just because these two men had on gray uniforms—"

"I know," nodded Clay glumly. "My ears feel long and fuzzy enough about it without you reminding me."

"Cheer up," Tryon rallied him. "This little adventure gives you the chance to meet one of the greatest men alive today. Wagner, step out and ask the corporal to see if General Grant has a minute to spare for us."

Wagner departed. Tryon inquired after the health of Shadburne, Dulin, Hugh Scott, and others, as though they were relatives or dear friends. He asked if Clay had seen Lark Winstead recently, and spoke of his admiration for her. The spectacled corporal returned and saluted.

"General Grant desires that the prisoner be brought," he said.

"Very good. I'll walk ahead. Stay behind Buckner, Corporal, and keep your finger on the trigger of your revolver. Buckner has many excellent qualities, but he's not anxious to enjoy our hospitality."

They came out into the big room, and Tryon opened another door. He led the way along a corridor beyond. Doorways opened into busy offices on both sides. At the end of the corridor Tryon knocked at the last door. A voice spoke from inside, and Tryon opened the door and ushered Clay in before him.

The office in which Clay found himself was a long, narrow one, its walls covered with maps. Two desks stood together at one end, with uniformed clerks busy at them. At the other end was a table at which sat a small man with a short dark beard and a shabby blue blouse with three-starred shoulder straps. Beside his elbow was an empty plate, as though he had just finished eating while he worked. Out of his beard jutted a glowing cigar, and his wiry hands were full of papers. He glanced up as Tryon escorted Clay toward the table.

"General," said Tryon, "permit me to introduce Clay Buckner, of the Rebel Iron Scouts."

Clay drew himself stiffly to attention and saluted.

Ulysses S. Grant took the cigar from his mouth and lifted his right hand to his brow in a return salute. "Buckner," he repeated, in a flat, businesslike voice. "Well, Buckner, are prisoners allowed to salute in the Confederate army?"

"General Grant," replied Clay, still at attention, "I must respectfully decline to answer any questions whatever about the Confederate army."

Tryon seemed to gulp and choke beside him, as though stifling a laugh. Ulysses S. Grant actually smiled, very tightly and harshly, with his lips close together in his beard.

"Colonel Tryon, this man is mighty ready-tongued with everything but information," he said.

"That's the Iron Scout way, I'm afraid, General," said Tryon.

Grant's eyes were again on Clay. They were blue-gray eyes, as steady as two gun rests, and seemed to burn their way into Clay's mind.

"You're in Federal uniform," Grant said gravely. "Of course you realize that you can be hanged for wearing it."

"I do realize it, General," responded Clay. "And of course you, sir, realize that if I'm hanged my friends will instantly hang a prisoner to make things even."

"I can vouch for that policy of theirs," offered Tryon respectfully.

"I know, I know," said Grant, putting his cigar back into his mouth. He clamped it in his teeth and spoke around it.

"As a captured spy in Federal uniform, you are aware of your dangerous situation," he went on. "You might improve your lot by answering some questions."

"Probably I could, General Grant," was Clay's reply, "but I won't. I repeat, I must respectfully decline to give any answers."

"Where are the headquarters of the Iron Scouts?" Grant asked him.

"I'm sorry, General. I have nothing to say."

Grant's gaze shifted to Tryon. "This is what you've given me to expect of the Iron Scout service, Colonel. What do you suggest?"

"Since you honor me by asking, General, my advice is to lock him up under guard."

"Exactly," nodded Grant. "You may do so, Colonel Tryon." Again he fixed Clay with his level stare. "Buckner, you'll be shut up alone. You'll have a chance to think things over. Maybe you and I can talk to more purpose tomorrow."

"I fear not, General," said Clay, still braced at attention.

Again Grant half smiled as he bit on his cigar.

"That's all for the present," he said. "Take him away, Colonel."

Out went Clay, escorted by Tryon and the corporal. They walked along the corridor, waited in the big outer room while Tryon and the corporal found hats and coats, then emerged in the chill winter night.

"Well, Clay," said Tryon, "what do you think of General Grant?"

"He seems right civil and right soldierly," replied Clay. "What do you think of General Lee?"

"I hope I never get into his grip the way you are in General Grant's, Clay. Come on, it's cold out here and I'm going to put you away nice and cozy."

The three of them walked in the darkness, along a well-trampled path past the rear of the big headquarters building to a huddle of smaller structures behind it. One long, low shed faced away from the river and the other buildings, toward wintry trees. It showed a row of barred doors, with lanterns hung to the eaves in front of them. As Clay and his escort made their way along the front, men looked out through the bars.

"This is a special hotel for guests we want to keep close to us," Tryon told him. "Unlock that last cell, Corporal."

"It's already open." The corporal swung the door wide, and Tryon gestured for Clay to enter. The door closed behind him.

He was in a narrow compartment, little more than six feet wide by eight long. At the far end, under a tiny iron-grated window, was a bunk spread with blankets. Beside it was a stool, and in one wall there was a fireplace with a small but warm blaze.

"Where's that sentry who's going to be on duty here?" Clay heard Tryon asking outside.

"He's on his way here now, Colonel," said the corporal.

Clay went to the bars of the door and peered out.

Tryon stood under a swinging lantern as a slim pink-faced soldier approached, musket on shoulder. The man stopped and saluted by bringing his left hand to the lock of the musket.

"What's your name, sentry?" asked Tryon. "Oh, it's Chadwick."

"Yes, sir."

"Very well, Chadwick, this particular cell and the man inside it are your most important charge. The lock's defective—can't be closed—and I don't want to come back and find he's escaped. He's General Grant's particular prisoner."

"Yes, sir," said the sentry called Chadwick, and looked in at Clay. He looked young and smooth-skinned, and his eyes were round and blue. "That him?"

"He's the only one in there, isn't he?" said Tryon, rather sharply. "All right, Chadwick, take over."

Chadwick saluted again.

"I'll see you later, Clay," promised Tryon. "Come on, Corporal."

They departed, going out of Clay's sight.

≽ 5 ≼

Flight and Pursuit

"That strutting skunk!"

It was the sentry, speaking between his teeth as he watched Tryon's departure. His face had crinkled out of its smoothness, his pale blue eyes had narrowed.

"Who are you talking about?" asked Clay, lounging at the barred door.

"Colonel Tryon, that's who. He talked to me like I was the dirt under his feet."

"Oh," and Clay laughed. "He's not as bad as that. As a matter of fact, I rather like him."

The slim young sentry turned a questioning eye upon Clay. "Like Colonel Tryon? But you're a Confederate."

"Certainly. And he's a Yankee. We've been at each other's throats time and time again, but I find a lot in him to admire."

"You don't have to serve under him," reminded the sentry. "You don't know how hard he works his men and how little he cares about them."

It was Clay's turn to be surprised. "I thought things

46

were easier here at headquarters than out on the battle front."

"That's what I thought when they sent me here, but I've wished to be with a fighting regiment again and again, with only bullets to sniff at me."

He poured out a grumbling flood of complaints about long hours of duty, refusal of furloughs or even brief relaxations, insistence by Tryon and others on painfully clean and correct uniforms, arms, and equipment.

"Why did you join the Union army?" inquired Clay.

"For the bounty," was the sentry's reply. "In my town they were offering a hundred dollars for recruits, so I enlisted. And six hours after I'd been sworn in, I heard that the bounty in the next town was fifty dollars more."

Clay laughed, and the sentry gritted his teeth.

"That's been my luck from the first—being cheated out of things. You know something, Johnny Reb? I wouldn't mind changing places with you."

"With me?" cried Clay. "Do you know I'm here because I'm accused of spying?"

"Well, at least you can sit down," said the sentry enviously. "You get your meals brought to you, and you can sleep as long as you want to tomorrow morning. And you aren't going to get hurt—I know all about how they don't hang Iron Scouts. The war's over so far as you're concerned. I'd settle for a nice cozy nest in a cell, or maybe a discharge from the service."

An aproned, shirt-sleeved cook's helper appeared

outside the door with a big steaming bowl in one hand and a huge iron mug in the other. "Here's some supper," he called cheerfully through the bars. "Get this door open for me, sentry."

"Aw, open it yourself," the sentry growled. "The lock's no good."

Clay shoved the door open, and received a bowl of chicken stew and the mug of coffee. The cook's helper departed, and the sentry sniffed with grumpy relish.

"That's officers' rations they gave you," he said. "Know what I'll get when I go off duty here? Beans and sowbelly, sowbelly and beans. Not fit for a dog. I could use some of that coffee; it's getting mighty chilly out here."

"If you've got a cup, poke it in here," invited Clay. "I'll give you some of this; there's a pint or more of it."

The sentry unslung a battered tin cup from his belt, and Clay measured half his coffee into it. They sipped together, on opposite sides of the grating, while Clay devoured the stew and asked questions.

His guard's name was Sim Chadwick, and among the other woes Sim Chadwick complained of were sore feet, dislike of hardtack, and a strong sense that the Confederacy might be right in wanting independence. Chicken such as Clay ate was never seen by the headquarters privates' mess, he said, and he hadn't had ham since he had left home.

"I've had side meat enough to freight a ship," he

said, "but I haven't seen a ham or a shoulder. Those pigs they sell the army must be two miles long."

"Hams and shoulders go to the officers," suggested Clay.

"Just what I was saying."

Sim Chadwick went on to speak angrily about high prices charged by sutlers, the coldheartedness of a girl in his home town who had written that she would marry another soldier, and, once again, the overbearing manners and methods of Colonel Tryon.

"My best friend, Chalk Newsom, let a prisoner get away from him last October," he remembered wrathfully, "and old Tryon put Chalk in the guardhouse for six days and then transferred him to the quartermasters', to drive mules." Suddenly the anger died out of his pink face and it lighted up with inspiration. "Hold on! Look here, Johnny, maybe you'd be willing to do me a favor."

"Favor?" repeated Clay. "What kind of favor?"

"Well, now," and Sim Chadwick pushed close against the bars and whispered, "what if you sneaked out of here and ran off while I wasn't watching? Then —don't you see what would happen? I'd get sent to the quartermasters', too. I'm pretty good with mules. I prefer 'em to colonels like Tryon, any day."

Clay looked at him calculatingly. "Well," he said after a moment, "you're asking a right much of me, but—"

"Psst!" broke in Chadwick. "Don't say anything

else; here comes my relief. I'll be back here on post, just before dawn. We can plan it then. Don't give me away."

"I won't," Clay promised him solemnly.

Outside, a detail of men marched up with muskets at the shoulder. They halted at the barked command of their corporal, and one of them stepped out to take the place of Chadwick, who fell in and went tramping away with the others. The new sentry was a thickset man with a pointed beard, who posted himself in front of Clay's door.

"That seems to be a right clever fellow, your comrade who was here just now," ventured Clay chattily.

"Prisoner," grated the new sentry formally, "my orders are to speak to nobody except in line of duty. If you have anything to say, I'll call the corporal of the guard to listen to you."

"Oh, I don't have anything to say," said Clay. "Good night."

He walked back into the cell, put more wood into the fireplace, blew out the candle, and sat down on his bunk. He drew off his boots, folded his overcoat and blue blouse, and laid them on the stool. Then he stretched out and pulled a blanket over him. He felt like relaxing, for all he was a prisoner and miles from his friends.

Twice before he had been captured by the Federals, he told himself, and twice before his amazing good luck had set him free again. That good luck seemed to be holding, this time most amazingly of all. Chadwick, the unhappy sentry, wanted to look the other way while Clay walked out. Was this a pretense, to trap Clay somehow? But it was Chadwick who proposed escape, not Clay.

He fell asleep, as soundly as though he had been in his own bed at home on the Buckner farm in North Carolina.

"Psst! Wake up in there, quick!"

Clay fairly leaped up from the cot. The fire had burned out, and it was frosty cold in his stone-flagged cell. Gray dawn peered in through the bars at the door.

"It's me—Sim Chadwick," came the conspiratorial voice from outside. "They just put me back on guard. Come on, if you're going to skedaddle out of here and give me a chance to get transferred."

"Give me a second, Sim."

Clay swiftly dragged on his boots and caught up his blouse, leaving his overcoat where it was. In the cloth of his blouse sleeve were sewn several gold pieces, and he ripped the stitching to pull out one of them. Chadwick was opening the door for him, very slowly lest the hinges might squeak. In a moment, Clay stepped out into the cold dawn.

"Take this," said Clay again, and thrust it into his hand. Sim Chadwick stared at the gold piece with blank blue eyes. Clay snatched the musket from him.

"I just don't want you to change your mind at the last moment and shoot me at close range," Clay said. He tossed the musket inside the cell, and it fell on his bunk. Then he caught Chadwick's sleeve and spun him around so that his back was toward the door. "Wait until I'm gone before you go after your gun. Then raise all the yells you want. And when you start shooting, I hope I'm too far off for a good aim."

With that, Clay put his head down like a sprinter and fairly raced for the woods beyond.

A dozen leaping strides had carried him almost to the nearest of the sheltering trees when a cry rose behind him.

"Help! There he goes—he's escaping!"

That was Sim Chadwick's sharp, shrill voice. Other voices answered with shouts, but Clay did not look back. He dodged in behind the first tree, ran around another, and in among more thickly grown trunks, even as a musket roared and a bullet slapped into wood somewhere near at hand. The voices jabbered excitedly on his track, and he made a high, strong leap to clear a stump, charged madly through a clump of bushes with thorns that scratched, and almost fell flat as he went splashing through a pool skinned over with ice. On he fled, and on.

"I'm covering ground mighty fast on foot for a man who's used to riding," he couldn't help joking in his heart.

But his pursuers were covering ground fast, too. They did not yell to each other now—they must be saving their breath. However, he heard them rattling branches in the woods on his back trail.

He himself was not running quite as fast now. That headlong burst of speed had taken the edge off his explosive vigor. He slackened his pace. The men after him would be slowing down, too. Before they narrowed the distance between themselves and him, he might have time for a ruse to throw them off his trail.

Ahead of him was a close-grown mass of young evergreens, little more than shrubs. He plunged into it and through, breaking branches and crushing needles. Coming out on the other side, he spun around swiftly and again hurried back through the way he had come. Then he ran with hopping strides to one side, ducking in among larger trees. There, he congratulated himself, that fresh-broken mark from his body would lead them through and beyond, while he avoided them and found a new line of retreat and ultimate safety.

But even as he paused to catch his breath, he heard them coming. They moved smartly but not at any headlong speed, and they were talking again.

"Here's where he went," spoke an instantly recognizable voice. "I don't have to be an expert to pick out his tracks in all this mud."

It was Tryon, directing the chase. How had he happened to be so close to the cells at dawn?

"Lead on, Chadwick," Tryon was saying. "Don't crowd him too much. You other men stay beside me. Corporal, head back and bring up horses for you and me, just in case we need to do some riding. The trail's getting dim again up here."

"Not to me, Colonel Tryon," spoke up Sim Chadwick. "I could follow a snake's track across a dry rock. He's heading straight for those evergreens."

"Keep on. You two infantrymen hold your fire and stay back," directed Tryon. "Follow Clay Buckner, but I don't want him caught yet."

Crouching where he had stopped, Clay frowned. Not catch him yet—why not? And Chadwick was acting as scout and trailer, he who had wanted Clay to escape so that blame and transfer would come to Chadwick.

"On through that little hedge, now," Tryon ordered.

"Wait a moment, Colonel." That was Chadwick again. "He didn't go that way."

"But look, he fairly tore through it!"

"Yes, sir, and then he fairly tore right back again. Look how the branches are bent both ways. He doubled back and went along here to the side."

"Right, Chadwick," praised Tryon. "You're as sharp-eyed as Daniel Boone himself. Come on, boys, after him."

They were heading toward where Clay lurked. Again he sprang up, better for his brief rest, and ran as swiftly as he could without telltale noise.

Almost at once he came out upon a clearing, and raced across it like a deer before they could come close enough to spot him in the open. He climbed a big spreading sycamore and ran out upon a thick, swaying branch. As he did so, he saw his hunters come into view in the clearing behind.

Chadwick and Tryon were there, each carrying a drawn pistol, and with them were two infantrymen with ready muskets. Clay went as far as he could on the branch, then leaped to catch the top of a tall sapling just beyond. His flying weight carried the sapling forward and down, and its bending broke his fall. He landed on the ground on his feet, a good dozen yards from where he had left it to swarm up the sycamore.

Again he ran with all his might, until his lungs began to hurt for lack of breath. Then he slowed to a walk. Perhaps he had shaken off those harrying Federals. A stream, narrow and swift, flowed across his way, and a log spanned it. He picked his way along the log and ducked among more trees on the far side. But again voices spoke behind him.

"That Iron Scout's a smart one, Colonel," Chadwick was saying. "He must figure we'll be on his track, and he's trying to leave as few traces as he can."

"If I know Clay, he'd be bound to do just that," Tryon replied. "But he doesn't know we have a master tracker like you along. What's happened to his footmarks now?"

"He crossed on this log, sir. I see mud from his boots flaked off on it."

"Take your time, Chadwick. We've got miles to go before he leads us to that den of Iron Scouts."

Clay fought back a despairing exclamation.

That was it, the explanation for everything—Chadwick's false avowal of hatred for Tryon, the offer of the chance to escape, this steady but not desperately close pursuit.

Tryon had planned and ordered the whole affair for the chance to follow Clay's tracks into the camp of Clay's friends and comrades.

≽ 6 ≼

The Tricking of Tryon

For one furious instant Clay felt a driving impulse to walk out into the open, his hands high in the air, saying that he surrendered and would go back to City Point. He actually chuckled to himself as he imagined the look of disappointed surprise on Tryon's side-whiskered face because Clay would not be leading his harriers to the camp of the Iron Scouts.

But then he dashed off again, swiftly and silently for all his mud-clogged boots, stooping low to keep his head from stirring the leafless branches of the forest. He ran straight eastward for a while because the place Tryon wanted him to show them was south by a few degrees west, no more than twelve miles away.

He came to the margin of the creek again, and speeded up and sprang across it, splashing the shallow water at the far side. He stamped with his boots deep in the mud as he headed back toward the Union lines below City Point, then sprang up on a half-rotten stump, from there to a big bare rock beyond, and on to another rock. He jumped down and ran eastward along the north bank of the creek until he found a mass of soggy trunks and brush that half dammed the current. Standing on this, he carefully washed the mire from his boots, and then picked his way across to the south bank. Beyond, he moved more carefully to eastward, leaving as few marks behind him as he could.

He was becoming used to the wilderness of trees around him, to the running and way-picking. When the creek led him abruptly to the brink of a great swampy stretch of black still water with drowned bushes growing in it, he stopped because he must. Behind him he heard smashing noises, as though Tryon's party had grown larger and more careless. With all his efforts, he had failed to shake them off his trail.

All in an instant, Clay made up his mind.

He ran to a place where the high ground was hard and did not take his footprints. From there he dived head first into the water.

It was so cold that it almost paralyzed him, but he grimly swam on under the surface. His groping hands found matted stems, and he cautiously put his head above the surface among some of the thick-grown bushes in the water. He could see through them toward the farther reaches of the lakelike stretch. It extended a long way, among cold-looking trunks and dense tussocks of dead water weeds. Putting his feet down, he found that he could stand on the bottom, with his head above the water. Carefully he waded and dragged himself along, behind and among the half-submerged bushes.

Tryon's voice sounded at the brink from which Clay had sprung. "Where did he go from here, Chadwick?"

"That's what I'm trying to puzzle out, Colonel," replied the thoughtful voice of Chadwick. "It looks like he must have jumped in and tried to swim across."

Tryon laughed. "Maybe it looks that way, but if I know Clay Buckner he'd never be such a fool as to try it. He'd die in the middle of that lake; it would stop the blood from running in his veins."

Chin-deep in cold water among the bushes, Clay felt as though his blood had already slowed its course from a run to a creep. He peered shoreward through a crisscross of trees. He could see Tryon and Chadwick and the two infantrymen with their ready rifles, all four peering across the lake in the cold winter light. Behind them stood the spectacled corporal from the headquarters at City Point, leading two horses by the bridles.

"You'd think that Rebel had taken wings and flown," the corporal said plaintively.

"Buckner's not ready to join the angels yet," said Tryon. "Not by sixty years or so."

"He might have climbed up somewhere," offered Chadwick. "He did that once before. Maybe he's up one of these trees."

"We'll look and see if he is," directed Tryon. "If anybody spots him, give a yell and fire a shot, but don't try to bring him down. Let him start running again so we can follow."

Tryon and Chadwick and the two infantrymen

moved apart from each other and walked slowly along the shore of the lake, peering into the branches over their heads.

Clay watched them take a dozen watchful steps, twenty. The corporal still waited where he was, holding the two horses. They were handsome cavalry chargers, each branded with *U S* on the hip. On each saddle was slung a carbine in a scabbard.

"Shall I come along, Colonel?" the corporal raised his voice to ask.

"No, stay there and hold the point where we last saw his tracks. Keep your glasses polished for a glimpse of him."

"Yes, sir."

Tryon and the others moved on their watchful way, prowling, and staring up into the trees. The corporal turned his back to the water and the horses, and gazed back the way he had come.

"Now," Clay whispered to nerve himself, "now or never."

He moved gingerly among the waterlogged bushes, closer and closer to the shore. As the water grew shallow, he stooped down behind cover, almost double. He came out on land within six feet of the horses.

A single water-splashing spring, and he had raked a carbine from its scabbard and pointed it.

"Drop those bridles," he ordered, in a low hard voice, and the corporal spun around, his mouth wide open.

"One yell out of you, and you've yelled your last,"

warned Clay. He hoped the carbine was really loaded. "I mean what I say, Yankee. I will shoot if I have to."

The corporal put up his hands. Holding the carbine ready in his right fist, Clay rushed close to him and snatched his revolver from its holster. He stuck it into the waistband of his dripping trousers, and with a frantic scrambling leap was in the saddle of the nearest horse.

"Hey!" That was Tryon, turning and hurrying back. Clay shoved the carbine muzzle almost against the corporal's spectacled face.

"Don't come any closer, Tryon," he yelled, "or I'll finish your man here!"

Tryon stopped where he was. "Are you going to take my horse?" he demanded. "First you refuse my hospitality, then you steal my horse."

"I'm taking both horses," Clay informed him, "and I won't lead you to the Iron Scout camp, either."

"General Grant's going to be disappointed not to see you any more," Tryon protested.

"Please present my excuses to him."

A shot rang out. One of the infantrymen had fired, and the bullet slapped into a tree within a yard of Clay.

With a loud yell, Clay kicked the horse's sides and at the same time brought down the barrel of the carbine across the back of the other horse. It sprang away, stung and startled, and galloped off among the trees. Clay rode swiftly away to westward.

He had headed back almost to the outer line of pickets around City Point before he found a well-trampled path through the woods. Along that he rode, westward and ever westward, for fully three miles. Let Sim Chadwick try to track him now, he exulted to himself, and turned his horse's head in among the trees again.

He traveled the rest of the way without further mishap. He shivered in his drenched clothes, but he felt comforted and secure when Hugh Scott and Bob Dulin rode out of a brush clump a good mile from camp, to ride silently up on either side of him to make sure that he was one of their own organization.

"You look kind of moist, Clay," said Scott. "What's the matter—you been swimming so early in the year?"

"How was the water?" added Dulin.

"Not anywhere near warm enough to scald a hog," Clay replied. "I had to jump in because some Yanks tried to follow me here. If they'd dogged me this far, you'd have been ready for them."

"Us, and a couple more of the boys within hoot-owl call," Scott told him. "Those Yankees wouldn't have found anything but trouble."

"How many were there?" Dulin asked.

"Five," said Clay. "Maybe more behind them."

"We'd have got that first five before they could ask each other what was going on," said Dulin with relish.

Then Tryon would have fallen, realized Clay. He was glad it hadn't happened.

"Gentlemen, hush!" Scott was saying as the three of them rode on together. "Is that one of the new Yankee repeating carbines you've got there?"

"I haven't taken time to look," said Clay, and drew the carbine from its scabbard again. "Yes, it is. A breechloader, with six cartridges in the magazine and one in the barrel."

"What Barney Hennegan calls a gun you load on Sunday and fire all week." Hugh Scott laughed.

"Let me see it," said Dulin, and leaned from his saddle to take the carbine from Clay's hand. He examined it, opened it, and shook the brass cartridges out into his palm.

"Fixed ammunition," he grumbled. "The Confederacy can't furnish that to us, just powder and ball. Anyway, my muzzle-loader throws a bigger chunk of lead, and throws it farther and harder."

Clay took back the carbine, reloaded it, then rummaged in one of the saddlebags of his captured horse. "There's a bunch of cartridges in here," he reported, and drew them out, counting as they rode. There were forty.

"Enough to run up a big score of Yankees in a hurry," said Bob Dulin. "Congratulations, Clay."

They reached camp, where Shadburne and the others welcomed Clay and listened with interest to his adventures as he got into dry clothes.

"We wondered if you hadn't stumbled into trouble, and we've been poking here and there for signs of what might have happened to you," said Shadburne. "So

Tryon's been asking about us, eh? And trying to come pay us a call, too." He laughed aloud, and stroked his brown beard. "You know, I can't help liking Tryon."

"I can't, either," admitted Clay.

"I always did think he was a good chap for a Northerner," added Scott.

"I don't like any Yankee," contributed Dulin.

Shadburne looked at Dulin and gave a little shake of his head, as though at a sulky boy. Then he addressed Clay again.

"You got back here just in time. We're going to break up camp."

"We are? Where are we going?"

"We're not supposed to know the answer to that," replied Shadburne, "but you know the Iron Scouts find out 'most everything. General Lee's cavalry corps is being split. Old Wade Hampton will go down to South Carolina to fight Sherman—he's heading up from Georgia, you know—and Butler's Division will go along. That means all the South Carolina and Georgia regiments. Most of us will follow old Wade."

"I'm a North Carolinian," said Clay.

"Yes, so you'll be assigned to stay here with the North Carolina troops. Fitz Lee—Marse Robert's nephew, you know—will command here, and you and Sloan will stay, and Bob Dulin, too, because he's a Virginian, and maybe one or two others."

Next dawn the Iron Scouts were up, packing their possessions and saddling their horses. They looked at the mud-plastered huts and the ashes of the fires, as though they were saying good-by to a happy, comfortable home.

"Now," said Shadburne, "one last duty." From his hip pocket he took a folded paper, and slid it into an envelope. "This is a letter to our old friend Tryon."

"To that Yankee?" demanded Dulin sharply.

"That's right. I'm going to leave it here," and Shadburne carefully wedged it in a split stick and thrust the stick upright in the central clearing. "One of the folks who lives here in the swamp—you remember him, Clay, his name's Walsh and he took us in last month when we got away from that Yankee barge at City Point—will come and pick it up, and see that it gets through the Union lines to Tryon."

"What are you telling him?" Clay asked.

"I drew him a map, showing him how to get to this place. He wanted to visit us so mightily, I thought I'd tell him how to come here. But we'll be gone. Come on, boys, mount and head for cavalry headquarters."

≫ 7 ≪

The New Service

As the Iron Scouts left their Blackwater lair for the last time, rain began to fall. It was a chill, shivery rain, but it helped them sneak through the Federal lines. Miles southward and through a string of cavalry pickets they found an unguarded path, wide enough to permit only a single file of riders to make its way. Beyond, they were challenged by South Carolina troopers they knew, and arrived in the camps of Wade Hampton's cavalry.

Things there were on the move, swiftly but secretly. Relatively few of the horses of Butler's Division would make the journey—Butler's men counted on finding remounts for themselves in their native South Carolina. Shadburne reported with the Iron Scouts to huge, dark-bearded General Hampton, and the cavalry chief soberly welcomed his prized scout.

"I asked for you and your men because I don't think the need for you here will be so great," Clay heard Hampton telling Shadburne. "The cavalry here will be reduced in numbers and drawn in toward Petersburg for service here and there along the line. Down yonder, we'll be out in the open and you can find plenty of scouting to do behind the lines of another Union army."

"I'm used to that kind of work, General," Shadburne said. "Do all the Iron Scouts go along?"

"No, each man reports to his original regiment for transfer. That means some will stay if their regiments are left in Virginia."

This decision would leave Clay Buckner and Jim Sloan of North Carolina, and Bob Dulin and two other Virginians. Hampton's move southward was set for the following dawn, and there were good-bys around the last campfire of the old organization.

"All the luck in the world, Clay," said Shadburne. "We've come through this far in the war, and I think we'll come the rest of the way through—most of us. Let's get in touch when the last shot's died away. I never want to forget my old war comrades."

"Take care of Grant up here," charged Hugh Scott, clasping Clay's hand warmly, "and we'll take care of Sherman down yonder in the Carolinas."

"Never forget you were an Iron Scout, wherever they put you," drawled Jack Shoolbred.

Farewells were the more quickly said because nobody liked to say them. Before dawn the next day Clay once more mounted Cherokee and he and Jim Sloan rode off to the lines of the First North Carolina Cavalry, while Dulin and his friends sought the Virginia regiments.

The tattered, bristle-bearded men of Company A

of the First North Carolina surrounded Clay, shaking his hand and slapping his back.

"Welcome back to the old One Horse!" whooped Windy Struble. "You never stayed with us more than about a day before you went off with them Iron Scouts to drink stolen Yankee coffee and wear stolen Yankee uniforms. You come back to see how real soldiering is done, huh?"

Captain Whitaker of Company A also shook hands, and spoke gravely.

"I wish we could keep you here, Buckner," he said. "We're not very numerous in Company A any more, and we could use somebody who knows how to ride and shoot the way you do. But Colonel Cheek has received orders concerning you."

"What orders, Captain?" asked Clay.

"Here they are." Whitaker handed Clay a blue-tinted paper from headquarters. "You and your comrade Sloan are both to report to the commander of the Second Corps."

"That's General John B. Gordon," remembered Clay. "What am I to do there?"

"My guess would be, more scouting."

On the following day, Clay rode Cherokee into the infantry lines west and south of Petersburg. With him went Sloan. Soberly they identified themselves to pickets, to sentries behind pickets, to provost guards behind sentries. The defenders of Lee's entrenched lines were gaunt as greyhounds, shaggy as sheep dogs. They wore fantastically tattered uniforms, and shielded themselves

against the cold with cloaks made of blankets or car-
pets, sometimes with captured blue overcoats such as
the Iron Scouts habitually wore. Many were without
shoes, wearing sacks or rags tied around their feet.
They would have looked like an army of forlorn tramps
if it had not been for their weapons.

Those weapons were another story. Their muskets
and rifles gleamed like the brave high hopes of the still
unconquered Confederacy. And their headquarters'
tents and huts flew the Confederate battle flag, bright
defiant red with a cross of blue and stars on the cross.
Many of the flags were torn by the bullets and shrapnel
of countless pitched battles, but they seemed to flutter
all the more defiantly in the bitingly chill breeze of
January. Officers at the headquarters were nearly as
shabby as their men; yet there was something about
those officers—the way their sabers swung from their
belts, the set of their hatbrims, the drape of their coats
around lean waists and straight backs—that made them
look like the best officers in the world.

Clay remarked as much to Jim Sloan, who nodded
sober agreement.

"I reckon they *are* near about the best officers in the
world," said Jim. "They don't have hair oil, or ten
pounds of gold braid, or patent polish for their old
boots, like the officers in the picture books. But they've
got near about four years of battle experience."

"Now that you speak of it," returned Clay, "you can
figure that these officers have come up, a lot of them,
from the ranks. We've lost captains and lieutenants and

colonels, and all the way up to brigadiers and major generals, shot away from in front of their commands. The best of the fighting men have had to take their places and keep moving up, and they've had to make good as officers the way they made good as soldiers."

"Like General Gordon himself," elaborated Jim. "I hear tell he didn't know what soldiering was before the war. He started in '61 by enlisting in a company they called the Raccoon Roughs. Doesn't sound elegant, does it? He was a captain when the Raccoon Roughs were mustered in, and he was a major at First Manassas. Then he got to be a colonel, and he was a brigadier general at Gettysburg. Now he's commander of the Second Corps, holding the right of these Petersburg trenches."

"I reckon the Yankee commanders have come up the same way," reminded Clay.

"I'm not studying about how the Yankee commanders came up."

They reached Gordon's headquarters on the banks of a narrow little creek. At one time those creek banks had been forested, but now only stumps showed where the trees had been cut away for hut-building and fire-making. To the north the creek flowed into the Appomattox River, and near the headquarters a trestle of the Southside Railroad crossed the creek. Gordon kept his office and sleeping quarters in a lean, rickety old farmhouse, with two rooms below and two above and a smoky chimney at either end. Behind the house stood a jumble of sheds and tents for staff and special service troops, and on the porch of the house paced a sentry. Clay and Sloan dismounted and offered their orders. The sentry jerked his head toward the door, and they entered.

A young staff officer with a bristly mustache studied the papers. "Ah," he said, "you've been expected. General Gordon himself will see you. Come this way."

They followed him into the other downstairs room. It was small and bleakly tidy, and there were a few coals of fire on the hearth. At a desk sat a slim bold-featured man, with a dark close-cropped beard jutting from his square chin and long black hair combed away from a high broad forehead. He glanced up, eyes intent and gray and hard as new bullets. Those eyes appeared three-cornered, set deeply in the hard-fleshed face. Clay and Jim Sloan instantly drew themselves stiffly to attention.

"General," said the aide, "here are the men from the Iron Scouts you asked for."

"Thank you," said General Gordon in a deep voice. "You may go, Captain." A strong soft Georgian accent softened his words.

The aide vanished. Gordon studied the papers, then looked up again.

"Which of you is Sloan?"

"I am, General," replied Jim. "This is Buckner."

"You look mighty young, both of you." Gordon himself did not seem old. Clay judged that his new commander was not much beyond thirty, for all the stars on his collar and the dimmed braid on his cuffs. "But if you're Iron Scouts," continued Gordon, "you've known what it is to play the man."

"We hope we've learned that, sir," said Clay.

"You're attached to my headquarters as couriers," said Gordon. "That's your new designation—couriers. Do you know what courier duty is?"

His eyes were on Clay, waiting for a reply.

"A courier carries messages and keeps headquarters in touch with other commands, General," Clay said.

"Well put, Buckner." Gordon's smile was somewhat fierce under his dark beard. "But where you two are concerned, the messages you'll carry will be through some right dangerous and debatable territory. And the units with which you'll keep these headquarters in touch will be yonder." He pointed southward. "On the Yankee side. In other words, you'll be called couriers, but you'll serve as scouts. Is that clear?"

"Very clear, General," replied Jim for them both. "And very welcome service."

"Good," Gordon snapped out. "All right, you may go now. The captain out there in the front room will assign you quarters." He rose, fully six feet tall, and vigorously sinewy for all his leanness. "I expect valuable service from you both."

He offered his long wiry hand to Clay, then to Jim. They shook hands, saluted, and left the office.

The aide escorted them out to the porch, where they took the bridles of their horses. Then he led them around to the back of the house and hailed a sergeant there.

"These men will be added to your detail, Sergeant Drumm," said the captain. "This is our sergeant of couriers, you two recruits. He'll attend to your billets and mess arrangements."

Sergeant Drumm was young, too, making the most of a fuzzy yellow beard like corn silk. As the officer departed, Drumm asked their names and shook hands as Gordon had done.

"He called you recruits, but you both look right seasoned to me," he said. "These horses of yours, they're mighty likely animals. I'd be glad to trade for that brown one, or I'd pay—"

"Sorry, Sergeant," broke in Clay at once. "Cherokee's not for sale to anybody, not to General Gordon himself."

"You ought to feel like that about your horse, Buckner. Well, lead those nags around here. The two of you can bunk in that hut at the end of the row."

It wasn't a bad hut at all, Clay and Jim decided; better, as a matter of fact, than those primitive shelters they had made for themselves in the soggy depths of Blackwater Swamp. This structure was perhaps ten feet square and was built of small poles laid hogpen style and chinked between with chips and twigs matted with clay. The inside had been plastered with a mixture of clay that was almost as good as mortar. The floor was of hard-tramped earth, and pine needles made two pallet-like beds against opposite walls. The roof was made of roughly split slabs lapped like shingles and thatched with more needles. There was a square window hole covered with the tattered half of a blanket, and a door made of two broad planks cleated together and hung on hinges of cracked leather. The chimney was also of sticks, well chinked and coated with clay inside, and the fireplace had a hearth of sooty stones.

"We're home, Clay," vowed Jim, tossing his saddlebags and blanket roll on one of the pine-needle beds. "If only I had a picture of my folks at home to stick up on the wall, now—"

"It'll be more homelike when we get a fire going," announced Clay. "I'll go out and rustle some wood."

"And I'll reap a little brush and make some kind of a windbreak for our horses," volunteered Jim. "That Yankee saber I brought along with me is going to do me some kind of good in this war, after all."

Clay had to range far and wide to bring in two or three pieces of thick log and an armful of smaller sticks for kindling. By the time he had made the fire and taken a battered bucket down to the creek for water, Jim had finished his rough brush shelter for his own horse and Cherokee.

"And now it's near about time to eat," said Clay. "Let's go hunt up our sergeant and draw our rations."

They sought Sergeant Drumm at the door of his own cabin, and made the acquaintance of half a dozen other couriers. Drumm dealt out supplies—dry corn, a tin cupful to each man, and skinny shreds of tough beef.

"Now, don't go drawing a long face at me," Drumm bade Jim Sloan. "I'm just a sergeant, not a magician, and I can't grab rations out of the air. Parch that corn on your fire, and hope your teeth are good enough to grind it. You get three more ears of corn for your horse, and a little bundle of hay—I feel sorrier for the horses than I do for the men."

"Do you think General John B. Gordon is eating any better than this tonight?" inquired a sunken-cheeked young courier, chewing a grain of his allowance of raw corn.

"Or Robert E. Lee?" put in another. "I've heard tell a report came in that Grant was so proud of his spies in Richmond and Petersburg that he said he knew what Marse Robert got for his breakfast every morning; and when Lee heard about it, he said that Grant couldn't know, or he'd send over part of his breakfast."

"We aren't complaining, friends," said Clay crisply. "We were just thinking that since we two are the newcomers we ought to treat you all to supper tonight."

"Supper!" groaned the hollow-cheeked one. "I love that word. But it ain't anything but a word around here any more."

"Just wait here, and we'll see what we can do," Clay told him. "Come on, Jim."

Back to their hut they hurried, and unbuckled their saddlebags. Clay got out a dozen big cakes of hardtack and three boxes of sardines, the trophies of a surprise raid on a Union sutler's wagon. From his blankets Jim unwrapped two big chunks of bacon, and chose the larger. They fairly ran back to Drumm's door and held out their offerings.

Tremendous Rebel yells shook the cold evening air.

"Where'd that plunder come from?"

"Christmas was done and past, I thought."

"Old Grant must be sending over part of his breakfast, after all!"

"Parcel it out, Sergeant," said Clay, dumping the things into Drumm's eager hands.

Someone produced a big well-whetted knife, with which Drumm sliced the bacon into generous shares for everyone. Each courier received two hardtacks, and the sardines were opened and divided equally all the way around. With joyous faces the hungry men sat down around a fire to munch.

"And boil this up for us to finish with," said Jim Sloan, holding up a paper package. "Coffee."

That word brought more cheers from the courier detail, so loud and prolonged that a clerk looked from a back window of the headquarters house. Everybody had a mug of black coffee, scalding hot and strong.

"Save all those bacon rinds," the sergeant warned. "This corn we didn't eat tonight I want ground up—there's a mill around here somewhere we used to use before we got too hungry to wait. And we'll fry out enough fat from the rinds to make us a batch of johnny-cakes for breakfast tomorrow."

Supper over and tin dishes washed, Clay and Jim strolled back to their quarters. The fire still burned, making the hut warm and bright inside.

"You held out something, didn't you?" Jim asked.

"Some more hardtack and a bottle of pickles and a

big slice of cheese," confessed Clay. "I was thinking that it might help out with tomorrow's dinner, after that johnnycake breakfast they're all looking forward to."

"Right, and my other flitch of bacon can go in," said Jim. "I reckon that between us we're just about feeding the courier squad for a full day. Day after tomorrow we'll share and share alike with them, on poor beef and parched corn."

⊱ 8 ⊰

Richmond

From the very first day of their attachment to Second Corps headquarters, Clay Buckner and Jim Sloan were under the personal direction of General Gordon. Staff officers or Sergeant Drumm himself sent other couriers to ride with orders, messages, and reports. But Clay and Jim found themselves hard at the work they knew from long and full experience with the Iron Scouts.

The Second Corps extended its lines well to westward of the main defenses of Petersburg, guarding the Southside Railroad. Since Fitz Lee had drawn in the remaining cavalry from its camps to the south, at last abandoning any effort to keep the Petersburg and Weldon line open, the Southside was the main supply line left open between the Confederate capital and the country still unoccupied by Union troops, and the Second Corps and the hard-working mounted forces were tirelessly on the watch against a Federal move to cut the Southside, too.

Clay and Jim habitually rode horses captured from the Union cavalry, each branded on the hip with a

U S, each with a McClellan saddle and a bridle of Northern army issue, each with a blue regulation saddlecloth and all other equipment from Union stores, down to the very halter rope. They themselves were dressed in jackets of Confederate gray, but wore blue breeches and overcoats so as to pass for Union troopers. Thus disguised, they made repeated rides to the west along the Appomattox River, past the far left flank of the Union forces, and then south and east on their scouting missions.

Clay found that the carbine he had captured when escaping from Tryon was his best passport through enemy pickets and patrols. Again and again he was stopped for questioning, but before he could dig his forged pass out of his pocket a corporal or sergeant would notice the breechloader slung in its scabbard at Clay's saddle. "Let him go," the order would come. "He's one of those scouts with the newfangled carbines."

He even rode into a work camp one day in February to ask for brass cartridges, as a pretext for gleaning information. The party was of Union engineers, rugged and knowledgeable men who were putting down a row of ties in a driving flurry of snowflakes, while gangs of their comrades laid rails upon the ties.

"We don't have any fixed ammunition here," said the officer in charge. "Hunt up a cavalry headquarters somewhere and let us alone. We're trying to catch up to our schedule."

"Schedule, sir?" Clay looked at the crew of tracklayers. Big men swung nine-pound hammers to drive in spikes that held the rails to the ties. "Military railroad, eh?" he suggested.

"You must have been spending a long time out there at the western edge of things," said the officer. "How is it that you don't know about what we're doing?"

"I've just reported from Sheridan's command in the Shenandoah Valley," Clay quickly replied.

"We've run this line all the way from City Point, across that Weldon Road we took away from the Rebels, and in a few days we'll be able to run supplies by the trainload out to your part of the lines on the far side of Petersburg. And nobody's told you a thing about it?"

"Nobody tells a private soldier anything, sir," Clay said plausibly. "But I'm glad the railroad's coming. That means plenty of hot coffee and warm blankets in this cold weather."

"Right you are," nodded the officer. "Who was it called this part of the world the sunny South, far away from all the ice and snow? Well, ride on now, I don't have any time to stand here gossiping with you."

Clay departed at a trot, doubled back, made the detour around the Federal flank, and reported to Gordon the following morning. His general listened, with quick, fierce nods of his head.

"That railroad means that they'll be able to run men and supplies all the way around us and concentrate on breaking the Southside line as soon as the weather lets up," he said. "I wish I could chop them off somewhere.

Make me a report in writing, Buckner, and then hold yourself ready for another ride."

Clay set down all his findings and presented them. Gordon handed the report to his adjutant.

"Copy those, Major," he directed. "Buckner, I'm sending you to Richmond with this news to present to the office of Adjutant General Cooper. You'd better be the one to carry it, because they'll probably want to ask you some questions. That fine horse of yours, the one you call Cherokee, ought to make the trip with you as fast as any passage on those slow, creaky trains they run from Richmond to Petersburg. How soon can you be in Richmond?"

"If I leave now and there's no new snow to block the roads, I should be there well before sundown, sir," replied Clay confidently.

"Then get ready to go as soon as we have the copy of your report to send along. You may spend tonight in Richmond. Write Buckner a pass, Captain. And, Buckner, I'll expect you back here by tomorrow at sundown."

"Yes, sir."

Clay saluted and went out to his hut. He exchanged his Union overcoat and forage cap for the gray coat and broad hat he had brought up from home. Saddling Cherokee, he took the report from Gordon's adjutant and rode off for the nearest crossing of the Appomattox.

Cherokee traveled bravely and swiftly through a

little sprinkle of snowflakes, accomplishing thirty miles before midafternoon. They crossed a bridge over the James River and entered Richmond.

The town was shabby, and its streets hummed with a sort of brisk, tense mood of industry. Straight to the headquarters of Adjutant General Cooper Clay rode, and was ushered into the presence of General Cooper himself.

The adjutant general of the Confederacy was bald on top, with waves of white hair above his ears, and his strong-featured face was cleanly shaven. Clay remembered that Lark's grandmother had spoken of Samuel Cooper as a young lieutenant long ago, gay and handsome and a social favorite. With Cooper sat a plump man in dark, spruce civilian clothes. This man's broad face was at once good-humored and shrewd. Clay recognized Judah P. Benjamin, the Confederate secretary of state.

Cooper took Clay's report, read it quickly, and handed it to Benjamin. Then Cooper fixed his blue eyes on Clay.

"You saw this railroad work with your own eyes?" he inquired.

"Yes, General, and I spoke to the officer in charge of it," said Clay.

"Oh, did you, indeed? And what did the two of you talk about?"

Benjamin and Cooper listened as Clay described his conversation with the engineering officer. When he had finished, Cooper looked as sternly fierce as had Gordon.

"That string of iron rails can hem us in completely," said Cooper.

"I was thinking that," agreed Benjamin. "I'll tell President Davis about it tonight." He looked back at Clay. "I remember seeing this young man somewhere —about a year ago, I think."

"Mr. Secretary, you saw me at an evening of charades last spring," volunteered Clay.

"Yes," said Benjamin, "now I remember. You appeared in one of the tableaux. You're in a vastly different field of endeavor now, my boy."

"I was present at those charades to catch a spy, Mr. Secretary."

"Yes," said Benjamin again, and smiled reminiscently. "A Yankee named Tower, masquerading as a Confederate major, and a very charming lady by the name of Parmenter. They were smuggling information through our lines to Washington. Well, Buckner— that's your name, isn't it?—Buckner, you're to be congratulated for that success. And for your success in scouting this new military railroad enterprise of the enemy."

"Thank you, Mr. Secretary," said Clay, trying to sound casual and modest.

"My compliments, too," seconded Cooper. "Wait outside while I write an acknowledgment for you to take to General Gordon. If you wish, you may billet tonight with the enlisted men of the staff here."

"Thank you, General Cooper, but if it's possible I

should like to call on some friends of mine in Richmond. Dr. Winstead, in the hospital service, and his family."

"Of course," said Cooper. "That's all, except for the dispatch for General Gordon."

When the message was given him, Clay stowed it in an inside pocket and rode off in the dusk of evening to the home of Dr. Winstead in northern Richmond.

He tied Cherokee to the hitching post before the pillared brick house, mounted the steps, and swung the big knocker at the door. Inside, a light showed in a window and grew brighter, as though someone carried it toward the sound of knocking. Then the door opened and Lark Winstead was there, lifting high a candle in a brass sconce.

Her blue eyes grew wide, and her mouth opened in amazed delight.

"Clay Buckner!" she cried out, and flung her free arm around him to draw him into the house. Her soft cheek cuddled his. "When did you get here?" She was so close she almost deafened him.

"Not so close to my ear, Lark," he begged, "and don't set me afire with that candle. I'm just in town overnight; I'm due back at Second Corps headquarters tomorrow. I wanted to see you and Dr. Winstead for a moment."

"A moment?" she echoed protestingly. "If you're going to be in town overnight, you'll be our guest here. Grandfather will get here in a few minutes, and he'll not hear of your staying anywhere else."

That was what Clay wanted to be told, and he did not argue. "Let me go out and put Cherokee under some sort of shelter," he said.

"We have an old carriage shed out back, but no feed. We don't keep horses."

"I always carry a few ears of corn with me."

"All right, you look after Cherokee. Then I'll let you in at the back door."

Clay returned to the street and led Cherokee in past the house. There was a snug shed behind; it would be welcome living quarters for any man in the Second Corps, he told himself as he brought Cherokee inside. Cherokee whinnied softly and gratefully as Clay unbuckled the saddle and bridle and put them away, then found an old blanket to drape over the brown flanks and fetched water in a leaky wooden pail. From a tow sack he took out several ears of corn for Cherokee's supper, then walked to the back of the house.

Lark let him in at the kitchen door. It was warm in there, with a fire crackling in the big iron stove beneath a steaming kettle that sent off a pleasant appetizing smell. The candle stood on the table.

"Smoked pork shoulder and fritters for supper," said Lark. "And I've got coffee ready."

"Coffee?" repeated Clay.

"Well, it's what we've been calling coffee in Richmond. I picked up the acorns myself, under the oak trees out there along the street, and roasted them brown and grated them." She poured a cupful from a pot and gave it to Clay, then filled a cup for herself. "And I made these candles, too, from tallow and beeswax mixed."

He looked at her. She wore a dark dress, worn and mended, with a white collar and white cuffs. Her thick black curls hung upon her shoulders. Gazing, Clay smiled.

"What are you looking at, Clay?"

"Just the spirit of the Confederacy in February of the fifth year of its independence," he said.

"Sit down here at the kitchen table."

They took chairs opposite each other, sipping the sham coffee.

"I'm sorry not to be bringing something to you," he apologized. "I mean the sort of things I used to be able to grab from those Federal camps when I was in the Iron Scouts. But when the service broke up, I gave everything I had to the boys at my new post."

He told her about the division of Shadburne's scouting force and his transfer to Gordon's courier squad next to the Southside Railroad. She listened with smiling interest.

"You and Jim Sloan did exactly right, sharing your last decent food out like that," she praised him. "As a matter of fact, I'd feel guilty if you'd brought it here instead."

He drank more acorn coffee. "This is good," he said.

"Oh, it's awful, Clay," she laughed. "You know it's awful, and so do I. But it just tastes good because we're here together."

"That's the truth," he said.

They heard slow footsteps in the front of the house, and hurried there. Dr. Winstead had come in, leaning heavily on his cane and limping more noticeably than Clay had ever seen him. He looked thin, and his hair had become snow-white. Clay helped him off with his gray cape, and the doctor unbuttoned the coat of his surgeon's uniform. He sighed wearily.

"Clay, you're thrice welcome," he said. "It does me good, at the end of this long, trying day at the hospital, to see a friend's face. Lark, my dear, we must invite Clay to supper."

"I've already done that," she said, "and he's going to stay here tonight. Now I've got to hurry to make those fritters. We don't have any servants this winter, Clay, so we've closed off the upper story of the house, to save firewood, and I do the housework between the times I help at the hospital."

They ate together, the three of them, at the kitchen table. Lark forked fritters onto Clay's plate, and Dr. Winstead sliced for him a portion of savory smoked shoulder meat.

"Dab or dwiddle, Clay?" asked Lark, dipping a spoon into a china jar of syrup.

"Not knowing what that means, I can't say."

"All right, I'll give you some of both. Here," and she put a spoonful of syrup on one fritter, "is a dab. And this," she added, the spoon quivering to scatter gleaming tawny droplets on another fritter, "is dwiddle."

"Sounds like fancy Virginia talk to me," he laughed. "You forget I'm a plain North Carolinian."

"From Northampton County, short miles from the Virginia border," Dr. Winstead reminded him.

"Doctor, I was brought up to believe Virginia was a sort of colony of Northampton County," joked Clay, and they all laughed, happy to be together.

Eating, they talked about Clay's parents and Lark's grandmother and aunt, still at the Buckner home. Clay told about Gordon's headquarters and his duties as a courier assigned to scouting. They finished with cups of the acorn coffee, as ceremoniously as though they had done justice to an elaborate banquet of the world's rarest and most appetizing delicacies.

"I am especially glad you came to us just now," said Dr. Winstead, lighting a cigar, "because we're leaving Richmond."

"Leaving Richmond, sir?" echoed Clay, surprised.

"I'm being ordered to duty in your own state, at Raleigh," the doctor explained. "My orders came through yesterday. With the campaign developing south of there, the government has established a big new hospital at Raleigh, and I've been assigned to take charge of it."

"And Lark will go with you?"

"No, Clay," and the doctor shook his white head. "It can be a touchy little matter, slipping through those Yankee lines to go to Raleigh, and I don't dare expose Lark to any danger. So I'm sending her away to a place west of here where the war hasn't touched as yet. To the home of an old friend of mine, Major Wilmer Mc-Lean."

"I go to the McLeans next week," said Lark, "and I'll ride on that Southside Railroad, past your camp."

"Wave to me as you go past," Clay said to her. "Who is Major Wilmer McLean, Doctor?"

"I used to know him when he lived near Manassas Junction," replied Dr. Winstead. "Well, the first battle of Manassas began by a Yankee shell dropping down his chimney and blowing up his stove. After the fighting was over, he decided he'd had a great plenty of war, enough to last him all his life. So he moved his family down to another piece of property he had, where he felt the war would never come."

"That was wise," said Clay, "because they had the second battle of Manassas in his old front yard the next year, and lots of fighting near there since. And Lark's going to him? I'm glad she'll be where the war won't reach. Where's Major McLean's new home?"

"At a place called Appomattox Court House," said Lark.

❧ 9 ❧

Robert E. Lee

Clay slept that night on a sofa in the Winstead parlor, with a comforting blaze in the fireplace. Next morning he was up before the winter dawn in time to have breakfast with Dr. Winstead, who would be off early for his hospital service. Lark served them with salt fish and hominy and more acorn coffee, and after Dr. Winstead had said good-by Clay helped Lark with the dishes. Then he went out and saddled Cherokee and led him to the kitchen door for a last word.

"I'll wave when I ride past your Second Corps head-quarters on the train," Lark promised. "I don't know exactly when that will be, but I'll wave, just in case you're there watching for me."

"You don't know how glad I am you're going to a safe place," Clay said earnestly.

"Well, Appomattox Court House sounds safe. It's such a small place that it isn't important to either army. And it's not on the road to anywhere, so armies won't be marching through. It's a sleepy, quiet little town in the midst of sleepy, quiet country. The nearest big town is Lynchburg, about fifteen or twenty miles west of there."

"And Lynchburg's held by the South," elaborated Clay, "and the southern end of the Shenandoah Valley's so full of snowdrifts that little Phil Sheridan can't come raiding to Lynchburg."

Lark took hold of Clay's weather-roughened hand. "Clay, I don't intend to say that I wish you were going somewhere safe, too. I know you don't want to be anywhere, doing anything, except where and what your duty is in this war. But I have faith that you'll be all right. I've always felt that there's some special protection over you."

"If you believe that, Lark, so do I."

They kissed each other, and Clay mounted and rode away southward to find the road back to Gordon's headquarters.

Clay was away again behind the Union line of works, studying the progress of that growing military railroad, when Lark went westward on the train late in February. It was Jim Sloan, kept at headquarters by a wound in his thigh, who gave Clay the news.

"We boys on the ailing list have taken to hobbling out of our quarters whenever a train goes by," he reported as Clay rubbed his horse down outside their hut. "This particular train was cranky and wobbly; it limped near about as bad as I'm doing this minute. While we were watching, some of the folks made signs to us from the windows. Then I saw Miss Lark Winstead, half out of her open window in the cold air with cinders raining all over her. She had a handkerchief, and she swept it back and forth over her head like one of those signal flags. When she spotted me—I got out in front of the others, and had my hat up on the end of this old hickory stick I hop along with—she yelled something I couldn't hear, and threw out the handkerchief. It had a stone in it to weigh it down, and this letter, with your name written outside."

He handed Clay a sheet of paper folded twice and stuck shut with candle wax. Envelopes were almost nonexistent in Richmond, Clay remembered as he broke the makeshift seal and spread Lark's letter out flat.

Dear Clay,

I write this as I'm getting ready to leave. Grandfather drew me a little map to show me exactly at what point we'll go past General Gordon's headquarters. I'll watch, and see if I can't toss this out to you.

I would object to being sent away from Richmond if I didn't realize that perhaps the food I've been eating will do more good to a brave soldier in the Petersburg trenches or a sick or wounded man in the hospital. Meanwhile, we'll be far apart, you and I—it's eighty or a hundred miles from Appomattox Court House to the western end of those breastworks around Petersburg, and right now that seems as far away as the moon.

I'll write to you as often as I can, but I won't

expect to hear from you except when you find an odd moment to drop me a line. When we parted, you looked as solemn and grim as ever I saw you, but you didn't show that you thought of giving up the war. I can't help but feel that, while the South has men like you, our cause is still strong and brave.

God bless you always, Clay. You know that I will be thinking of you, here where I write and on the train, and at Appomattox Court House.

Love,
LARK

"Golly whiskers, Clay," said Jim Sloan as Clay finished reading, "you look ready to whip the whole Yankee army single-handed. Are you mad at something?"

"Not mad a bit, Jim," said Clay, folding up the letter to put it away. "As a matter of fact, I feel fine. Got any paper? I want to write an answer to Lark."

He wrote that he was safe and well, and that she was not to worry unless she heard definitely that something had happened to him. He added his prayerful thanks that she was on her way to safety, far away from the battlefield where he remained. In the office of General Gordon's adjutant he begged an envelope in which to seal the note, and addressed it to Miss Lark Winstead, care of Major Wilmer McLean, Appomattox Court House, Virginia.

Then he returned to his task of scouting the railroad. On the last day of February he journeyed for miles along the way eastward behind the far-flung entrenchments of Grant's army almost all the way to City Point. In the familiar region around the head of the Blackwater, Clay conducted himself with double prudence lest some one of his former captors should meet him and recognize him; but he was able to map the course of the railroad there, and saw that it ran close to an old line of Confederate trenches that had been developed and strengthened into a trio of Union forts, close behind the main line and designed to support it in case of a strong Confederate attack.

Back he came safely once again, to offer his report and the rough map to General Gordon. On the night of March 2, Clay was sound asleep in his blankets on the pallet of pine needles. He woke to the sounds of his name shouted aloud and the insistent rattling of sleet on the boards of the roof.

"What's the matter?" asked Clay. "What time is it?"

"One-thirty in the morning, Buckner, and time for you to get up. General Gordon wants you at once."

Hurriedly Clay struggled into his uniform, pulled on his boots, and dashed cold water from the bucket onto his face. He took his hat and overcoat and came out into the chill sleet storm.

"Never mind saddling your horse," said the voice of Sergeant Drumm. "The general's in a mighty big hurry. Take my old plug; he'll carry you well."

"Thanks."

When Clay entered the front room of the headquarters house, Gordon was buckling on his saber. He nodded to Clay and took hat and coat from hooks on the wall.

"You're coming with me to General Lee's head-quarters," he informed Clay. "If he wants us at this hour, it's of the utmost importance. I want you with me because the general's asking about that Yankee rail-road."

The ride to General Lee's camp was not far, but it was dark and cold and blustery, and twice Clay was forced to mop away the sleet that had started to freeze to his eyebrows. General Lee and his staff occupied a big square house on the very shore of the Appomat-tox, and overcoated orderlies waited on the porch to take the horses.

"Wait here until I call you in, Buckner," com-manded Gordon, and entered, closing the heavy door behind him.

Moving close to the wall to escape the driving bombardment of icy particles, Clay found himself next to one of the orderlies. "What rank are you?" the orderly asked. "Sergeant?"

"A private," said Clay.

"What's a private doing here, calling on Marse Robert?"

"General Gordon didn't tell me."

"What do you guess you're doing here, then?"

"I haven't tried to guess," said Clay.

"You aren't very curious," chuckled the orderly.

"I'm just not very talkative," said Clay.

There was a wait of long minutes, cold and shivery and dark enough to seem like hours. Then the door opened, and light streamed out.

"We're ready for you, Buckner," called Gordon, and Clay entered.

At once he drew himself to attention and saluted, his heart thumping swiftly. Across the room, behind a long table with stacks and strewings of maps and papers, he saw the gray-bearded face of Robert E. Lee.

The commanding general of the Confederate armies was on his feet, a paper in his hand. He wore a military frock coat, its gray color only a shade darker than his hair and beard, and no insignia showed upon collar or sleeves. Clay saw that he was of more than average height, and strongly and finely made, with a ruddy skin and regular features.

Several times in the past Clay had seen his chieftain, at military reviews, on the march and in battle, but always at a distance. Now Clay was at close quarters, looking straight into Lee's brilliant dark eyes, and Lee was looking back at him.

"General Lee," Gordon was saying respectfully, "this is the young scout of whom I was telling you. He has seen that Federal military railroad closely and at first hand."

"He is young, as you say," observed Lee, his voice deep and gentle. "Younger than I had expected."

"Buckner's been tried in a very stern service, General," said Gordon, "and he's been found worthy of it. He was one of General Wade Hampton's Iron Scouts."

"Then he is brave," said Lee, his eyes still on Clay. "He is prudent, too, I hope."

"I can vouch for that, sir," Gordon said confidently. "He's been trusted with some of my most secret missions. Buckner, you're not to say one word about what passes here. Is that understood?"

"Perfectly, General Gordon," said Clay promptly.

"Good," Lee approved in his gentle voice. "Now, young man, General Gordon tells me of your observations along the rear of the enemy lines. I want to hear about them."

Respectfully and somewhat nervously, Clay described what he had seen and heard. Lee asked several questions, particularly about the railroad and its position in relation to the Union fortifications at the east of Petersburg. When Clay was finished, Lee bowed to him slightly but courteously, as though Clay were his equal in dignity and rank.

"Thank you," he said. "Now, General Gordon, we have already looked at these reports." He made a gesture toward the stacks of papers on the long table. "We have perhaps fifty thousand men in our trenches, not all of them really fit for duty. Grant has more than twice that, and Sheridan can bring twenty thousand more from the Shenandoah Valley. If Sherman marches up from the south without being halted by Johnston's army, he can add as many as eighty thousand."

He sat down behind the table, and at a motion from his hand Gordon took a seat opposite.

"Tell me frankly," said Lee, "what do you feel is our duty—yours and mine—toward our people and the army?"

Gordon cleared his throat. To Clay he seemed much younger—with his black beard and slim, hard figure —than his commander.

"General," said Gordon, as though speaking from long consideration, "it seems to me there are but three courses. First, make terms with the enemy, the best we can get."

He waited. Lee said nothing, but Clay saw him shift his head slightly, as though he meant to indicate refusal.

"Second, if that is not practicable," went on Gordon, "the best thing to do is retreat." He clenched his fist on the table. "Abandon Richmond and Petersburg, unite by rapid marches with General Johnston in North Carolina, and strike Sherman before Grant can join him."

Again he paused, and again silence fell in the room. Clay gazed raptly at Robert E. Lee. He remembered his audience with Grant six weeks earlier, when he was a prisoner at City Point. He had felt that the Union commander was an impressive man, an admirable soldier. But words like impressive and admirable were too dull to express Clay's feelings toward Lee. Here, he knew, was a leader to follow as long as one could draw another breath and take another step.

Lee was waiting for Gordon to continue, and Gordon did so.

"Or lastly," he said, "we must fight, and without delay."

"Is that your opinion?" asked Lee.

Gordon drew himself up fiercely in his chair. "Certainly, sir," he replied. "I came here at your order, I have answered your questions thoughtfully and frankly. Now, if you will permit me, I would like to ask your opinion. Do I have the right to do so?"

Lee actually smiled, kindly and understandingly. "Certainly, General," he said evenly, "you have the right to ask my opinion." He fixed Gordon with his dark gaze. "I agree with you fully."

"It is to be one of these three courses, then," summed up Gordon.

"Yes," said Lee. He shifted his glance to Clay. "Allow me to thank this young man for his services and for the clear description he has given us of the enemy positions."

"Buckner," said Gordon, "you may wait outside."

Clay saluted again. Lee and Gordon returned his salute. As Clay opened the door to leave, both generals were deep in earnest conversation again.

Back on the porch, Clay drew his coat tight and turned up his collar against the black cold of early morning.

"Well, soldier," said the orderly who had addressed him before, "you've been in right good company in yonder."

"The best," agreed Clay shortly.

"And what did those two generals tell you?"

"Among other things," said Clay, "they told me that I wasn't to say one word of what happened there."

The orderly whistled. "This Second Corps courier is almighty close-mouthed," he remarked to his companion who held the horses.

"A fellow gets close-mouthed in this army," said the other. "There's such a light issue of rations these days he forgets how to open his mouth to talk or eat, either."

Gordon came out at last, and he and Clay mounted and rode back toward their own headquarters. Gordon sat his horse silently, minute after minute. At last he told Clay to ride near to him.

"You're wondering what we decided after you left," he suggested.

"General Gordon, it isn't my place to wonder any such thing," Clay made haste to say.

"No, no. You've been taken into high confidence so far, and I'm going to take you into more confidence, because you're needed in what we'll do."

"Whatever you order, General," said Clay.

"I knew you'd say that. Very well, you heard me offer three courses of action, and you heard General Lee approve what I said."

"Yes, sir."

"We decided that we couldn't ask the enemy for terms," Gordon told him. "Terms are to be asked and received by civilian officials, not soldiers. And we aren't able to retreat from our defenses to join General Johnston, because we must hold Petersburg and the capital as long as possible. That leaves the third course."

"You said that was to fight."

"Yes," said Gordon, "to fight. That's what we're going to do. And I am to plan that fight, and you are to help me."

≫ 10 ≪

Fort Stedman

General Gordon was as good as his word. Clay found himself in almost daily conference with the Second Corps commander, and was sent on a variety of new scouting missions to observe as closely as he could the system of Federal trenches and redoubts that hemmed in Petersburg along the south.

Night after night that March, Clay crept forth from the Confederate positions toward the massive earthworks opposite. He found the distance between the fortified lines of the Army of Northern Virginia and the Army of the Potomac a short one indeed, and both stretches of defenses bristled with obstructions. In front of the Confederate parapets for mile upon mile lay trees that had been cut down, with the branches cut off short and the cut ends sharpened to form a nest of spikes to discourage any sudden advance. These makeshift fences were fastened together with chains and lengths of old cable from ships along the Richmond and Petersburg waterfronts, and the few narrow gaps through which a man could pass back and forth

were hard to find without directions. Adventuring beyond the sharp spikes in the narrow space between the
lines, Clay moved cautiously to avoid running into the
stealthy pickets of both sides.

He managed to crawl close to the Union works, and
there he found another forbidding arrangement of obstructions. The Federals had planted a close-set array
of stout wooden rails, each sharpened to a point and
with its butt set in a slanting pit so that it jutted in the
direction of Petersburg. Logs lay at the base of this
line of rails on either side, and the sharp rails were
bound to both sets of logs and to each other with stout
twists of wire. No man could shove through them or
leap over them. And they were set some six or eight
inches apart, the spaces between affording a good field
of fire for the Federals in the trenches on the far side,
should a Confederate attack be made.

While Clay thus carried out his scouting missions,
Gordon and the staff quietly moved the Second Corps
from its position defending the railroad at the west of
the defense lines to the trenches at the east. As his sparse
regiments arrived below Petersburg, the gaunt watch-
ers on duty there withdrew and moved across to take
their places. No one got any rest—General Lee had
perhaps forty thousand men fit for duty, and must
string them out on a front forty miles long. The
month of March continued cold and windy, and the
only action was by artillery, lobbing shells back and
forth like fiery-tailed rockets.

Gordon himself set up an observation post on a

high hill near his quarters, just behind Colquitt's Salient close to the eastern end of the line. He, his chief of staff Colonel Douglas, and other officers of his staff spent much time there with maps and field glasses. Again and again Clay was summoned to point out certain features of the landscape and the fortifications.

Gordon gazed through his glasses most frequently toward Fort Stedman, that massively bastioned strong point of the besieging army into which Clay had made an entry during January. Between Colquitt's Salient and Fort Stedman was a brushy stretch of ground, slightly hollowed and some hundred and fifty yards across. Upon it stood the neglected remains of an old cornfield. Fort Stedman was on a rise beyond this, with another rise to its rear. Stoutly defended emplacements for heavy guns were in plain view on either side of Fort Stedman.

"Who's in command at this point?" Gordon asked Clay on a gray, damp morning.

"Colonel Napoleon B. McLaughlen, sir."

"Napoleon," repeated Gordon. "He has a soldier's name, and he deserves it. I know his record. He has a brigade in the Yankee Ninth Army Corps, doesn't he?"

"A division, General. The First Division, with three brigades."

"What about the artillery over there at Fort Stedman?" was Gordon's next question. "Have you seen it?"

"Yes, sir, several times these last few weeks," replied Clay. "They're all big guns—rifled cannon and Coehorn mortars. Fort Stedman and Battery Ten to the east of it have eight companies of the Fourteenth New York Heavy Artillery. There are mortars and twenty-pounders in Battery Eleven and Battery Twelve, just west of Fort Stedman. Infantry are stationed in the trenches, and more infantry as a strong support just behind, on that hill you see."

"Yes," said Gordon, with his field glasses again at his eyes. "And on the far side of the hill, where that supporting infantry is—that's where their military railroad runs, eh?"

"That's right, General, with those three redoubts to defend it and support Fort Stedman. Yonder's the strong point of the whole Union position in this part of the country."

"The strong point," Gordon echoed him thoughtfully. "The last place of all where they'd expect us to hit them."

Clay glanced at his general, but Gordon was still staring off across the disputed ground and the shattered rows of dry cornstalks on it.

Jim Sloan, too, was drawn into the scouting assignment, making his own cautious observations of the Federal works, and he and Clay overheard from time to time the half-muttered talk of Gordon and his officers about the chances of assaulting and capturing Fort Stedman. They were not included in such conferences, and they took care not to discuss what they heard, even between themselves; but Clay, at least, developed a fair notion of the grand strategy of the coming attempt.

Gordon's Second Corps, reduced by now to no more than eight thousand infantry, would be joined by brigades from Longstreet's larger Third Corps, so that the column attacking Fort Stedman would approximate half of Lee's whole infantry force. In addition, a strong detachment of cavalry would be held in readiness, to follow in case the storming of Fort Stedman were a success.

On the night set for the attack, the obstructions of felled trees in front of the Confederate trenches would be removed as quietly as possible under cover of darkness. The charge across the intervening space would be pointed by picked men who would overwhelm the Union pickets and prevent them from warning their comrades in the fort, while other companies, chosen from among the strongest and most active of all the units, would hurry with axes to smash a way through the line of sharpened stakes that barred the way to Fort Stedman. A charge over the ramparts, as Gordon hoped, would scatter the artillerymen from their big guns, and the guns themselves could be turned to right and left to fire upon the Union positions alongside.

All this, according to Gordon's carefully laid plans, would be attempted in a single headlong rush. Even as that rush struck home at the fort, three more picked commands of one hundred men each were to speed on through and to the rear of Fort Stedman, pretending to be routed Federals. These would shout to the infantry in the supporting positions that the Confederates had flowed over the first line of works and that a retreat to the forts in the rear had been ordered. Penetrating to the three redoubts along the railroad, these forces would seize them and command the main line of Union defenses from behind. Then the infantry would move in both directions to clear the adjacent ramparts of bluecoats, while the cavalry would gallop through, gain the railroad, and destroy it and the telegraph lines alongside.

All this, if it should succeed, would mean that Grant's great blue phalanxes all the way along the lines to the west would be cut off from reinforcements and supplies and must fall back or be in dire danger. Then Lee could assume the active offensive, as so often before, and perhaps drive his larger but confused enemy headlong from before Petersburg and Richmond.

A desperate gamble, Clay told himself as Sergeant Drumm issued meager rations of corn to him and forage to Cherokee; but the situation itself was desperate. And Lee's army had won gambles before this.

Gordon's plans were complete. He waited only for a night without a moon and deep murky darkness in which to launch his grim lean regiments into action. And the last scrap of moon faded from the sky on the night of March 23.

On the following afternoon, the 24th, a letter came to Clay's makeshift shelter of mud-plastered stones and torn tent canvas. It was from Lark at Appomattox Court House, dated two days before.

Dear Clay,

It is so quiet and peaceful here that sometimes you seem a world away from me; at other times, it is as though I might speak your name and hear you reply. My hopes are with you and the brave army; that is all I can give—my hopes.

Today I got a letter from Grandfather in Raleigh. There has been fighting in North Carolina, as you must have heard, and he thinks Johnston's army is ready to fight at Bentonville. That means that he expects the hospital at Raleigh to fill up with wounded, both our own men and enemy prisoners. Meanwhile, he is delighted with North Carolina and has made many friends. Grandmother and Aunt Celie have managed to come and visit him. They think that we may all settle in North Carolina after the war, perhaps in some place not far from your home in Northampton County. Would you like that?

At any rate, it's something to think about and long for—after the war is over, whichever way it turns out. And even with all the desperate defeats, I cannot let myself think that it will turn out other than with our own final victory.

Love to you, Clay, from

LARK

Clay slept soundly that night, and woke in deep darkness. Unable to close his eyes again, he stirred up the little fire in front of the shelter and pulled out

Lark's letter to read once more. As he finished, Sergeant Drumm appeared in the firelight.

"General Gordon wants you," said the sergeant. "He always seems to want you around two o'clock in the morning; only this time he wants everybody else, too. I reckon the time's come for that jump at the Yankees, Buckner. Come along."

"Wait," said Clay.

He stuck a corner of Lark's letter into the little fire, let it blaze up, then dropped it. When it had burned out, he scattered the ashes with the toe of his boot. Then he picked up his breech-loading carbine.

"What was that you burned?" asked Drumm.

"Just a letter," said Clay. "Something I wouldn't want taken off of me if I got shot down or captured this morning before breakfast."

He went to report to Gordon, who returned his salute with a quick, businesslike downward snap of his hand.

"You'll stay next to me in this fight, Buckner," he said. "Have you had a bite to eat? There's some corn bread there on the desk. Help yourself, and go find your friend Sloan. We must be in the trenches as soon as we can get there."

Jim and Clay mounted their horses and rode after Gordon and his staff. Behind the line of entrenchments they dismounted. Jim and another courier led the horses along behind the party that moved on foot to the trenches. It was a chilly, foggy night, with the stars bright against the black sky overhead.

The trenches were muddy at the bottom, and as Gordon splashed in among the infantry he sank half-way to his knees, but he did not seem to notice. He questioned a major who stood among the men cradling their muskets in their arms.

"Has all that clutter of tree trunks and sharpened branches been cleared away from in front of us?" demanded Gordon.

"The work's being finished now, General," replied the major.

"Good. Now, pass this word to the officers who will command the men in this charge. The signal will come from in front of the parapet, a single shot. At that signal, every officer will order his men to climb up and rush. And if anybody fires before the signal, it will be considered disobedience of orders and will be severely punished. Is that clear?"

"Perfectly clear, General Gordon."

"Very well. Let those orders be passed along."

There was a long wait. Nobody spoke. Clay lounged against the cold earth of the trench wall, next to a towering bearded infantryman who puffed a corncob pipe as though he had no care in the world. At last the major returned.

"All is ready, General Gordon," he announced.

"Good," said Gordon again. "Keep the men on the alert." He raised his voice. "Sloan!"

"Here, General," said Jim Sloan from behind and above the trench.

"There's a point just to left of here where you can

bring those horses forward. As soon as the charge has left the trench, hurry them along and through for us to mount. Now, Buckner, you come with me."

Active as a boy, Gordon scrambled up the steep wall of the trench and over the parapet into the darkness. Clay climbed after him, his carbine in his hand. They moved forward together past several men who were lifting a big fallen trunk with sharpened branches, to set it aside. Beyond these men was a straggling patch of cornstalks, dried ears still dangling from them. Clay took time to wish he could gather some of those ears for Cherokee, who was on half rations like all the other Confederates defending Petersburg.

"When they've pulled that thing clear away—" Gordon began to whisper.

Just then one of the work party dropped the butt of the log, and it fell among dried twigs with a great thump and crackle.

"What are you doing over there, Johnny?" yelled a high, flat-toned voice from the direction of the Federal lines. It sounded only short yards away from them.

Clay heard the quick, furious catch of General Gordon's breath. A blue picket had come close, and had heard the noise of the falling log.

"What's that noise?" demanded the Federal insistently. "Answer quick or I'll shoot."

"Never mind, Yank," Clay called back. "Lie down and go to sleep. We're just gathering a little corn. You know, rations are mighty short over here."

A laugh drifted back to Clay, an understanding, friendly laugh.

"All right, Johnny, go ahead and get your corn," came the reply. "I'll not shoot at you while you're drawing your rations."

Silence again, and General Gordon's hard hand clapped Clay's shoulder in approval.

A soldier came toward them, moving with gingerly caution, his body bent almost double. "All clear for the charge, sir," he whispered to Gordon.

"Fire your gun and get them started," Gordon told Clay.

Clay lifted his carbine, finger on trigger, but hesitated. Near at hand, within a few hurrying strides, waited the unsuspecting Union picket who had agreed not to shoot at him.

"Fire your gun, sir," commanded Gordon again, his voice stern.

"Hello, Yank!" yelled Clay. "Wake up, we're coming!"

He fired the carbine at the stars.

A mighty roar shook the night, the chorused Rebel yell, and out of the trench boiled the attackers.

≫ 11 ≪

"Not Enough of Us"

To Clay the battle of Fort Stedman was, like so many other battles he had seen, a mighty swirl of confusion and a mighty thunderstorm of noise.

The headlong charge from the Confederate trenches swept past him and General Gordon in the darkness, and almost at once he heard the smashing blows of the axes on the slanting palisade of sharpened rails. Then another loud yell of fierce triumph as that obstacle went down and the infantry charged over its remains and straight up the parapets of Fort Stedman and the positions to right and left.

A group of mounted men came hurrying from the rear.

"That's my staff," said Gordon, and raised his deep voice. "Colonel Douglas! I'm here!"

The riders hurried close and reined in around Gordon and Clay. Jim Sloan was leading Cherokee and the general's horse. In a flash Clay and Gordon jumped into their saddles and rode off after the wave of attacking troops.

Ahead, the night was laced and ripped by flashes of gunfire, and the sound of the muskets was like the roll of a hundred drums all at once. As Gordon spurred up the slope to the very barricade, a wild yell saluted him and his companions.

"We have them!"

Clay sprang from Cherokee's back and down into the fort. Fires burned here and there on the floor of the trench, reflecting a red glow on the timber-faced banks of earth. Clay saw a knot of bluecoats, their hands in the air, guarded by two infantrymen. Beyond, a group of straining Confederates toiled to shift a great gun in its emplacement and aim at the flank. An officer appeared and saluted Gordon.

"We've taken this part of their works, General," he panted. "The only Yanks left alive right here are prisoners. We have Fort Stedman and a stretch of breastworks to either side."

"Nine heavy cannon," reported another man excitedly. "We're opening fire now on the enemy there to the east of us."

Even as he spoke, the captured cannon roared, full-throated. Its report shook the solid earth and its flash lighted the thick night. The loud Rebel yell beat up like an echo of the explosion.

"How many prisoners?" Gordon was prompting the first officer who had spoken.

"We don't know yet, but here's their commander."

The racket still reverberated around them as a bearded officer in blue stepped forward, guarded by a tattered Southern soldier with fixed bayonet. Gordon sprang down into the ditch behind the ramparts, peering closely. Another cannon boomed close at hand.

"You are—" said Gordon.

"Colonel McLaughlen," the prisoner identified himself. "I congratulate you on this early success, sir. But it won't last. This fight isn't over yet, not by a long way."

"No, not from all that noise," agreed Gordon. "I'm glad to meet you, Colonel. I am General Gordon, and I have the honor of relieving you of the command of Fort Stedman."

The Federal colonel was marched away. Other prisoners were hustled off to the rear toward the Confederate entrenchments.

"Sloan," said Gordon, "ride back to General Lee's position. I don't have time to write a dispatch, but I'll send one later to confirm your verbal report. Say to General Lee that we are in the enemy works at Fort Stedman and to right and left, and that our attack is continuing against the forts beyond."

Jim mounted and rode off. Gordon sat down suddenly on a box in the lee of the trench, while muskets flashed and barked all around. The general pressed his hand tightly to his arm just below the shoulder.

"You're wounded, sir," said Clay.

"Just a slight flesh wound," grumbled Gordon. "Does anybody here have a handkerchief or a scarf? Wad it up to stop this bleeding."

"You should go to the rear, General," said Colonel Douglas.

"Nonsense!" Gordon snapped. "They'd have to blow me in two to make me leave here now."

Another officer supplied a makeshift bandage, and Gordon strode away to direct the firing toward the second line of Union works. Clay kept at his heels. Then a messenger arrived at a run along the trench.

"I'm from General Lewis, up there with the advance," he said quickly. "They haven't found those forts along the railroad, and the whole Yankee army seems to be massing to push them back."

"That's bad news," Gordon groaned. "Douglas, where are you? Write a dispatch to send to General Lee. Here, Buckner, take the report and gallop back with it. We're halted here, but we'll hang on at Fort Stedman the best we can."

"Are you sending me out of the fight, General?" protested Clay.

"I'm sending you on an important mission," Gordon said. "That's enough for you. Obey orders, Buckner."

Clay took the folded paper from Douglas, scrambled up the parapet, and mounted Cherokee. The battle howled and crashed behind him as he rode back the way he had come.

He found his way to Lee's position in the rear of the salient from which the charge had been launched. Lee's chief of staff, Colonel Marshall, took Gordon's message. As he read it, he groaned almost as Gordon had done.

"Those three forts in the rear of Stedman must be full of Federals by now," said Marshall. "And the troops that were sent down from Richmond to reinforce Gordon can't get here in time—the railroad's broken down again."

Marshall hurried with the paper to Lee. Clay saw the gray-bearded commander in the dim first ray of dawn, intently reading. Then Marshall wrote swiftly at Lee's dictation, and returned to Clay.

"Take this back to Gordon," he directed. "It's an order for him to withdraw in as good order as he can manage."

Again Clay rode across the intervening space. As the light strengthened, shells were bursting wildly around Cherokee and him in the ragged remains of the old cornfield, but they reached Gordon in Fort Stedman without mishap to either of them. The commander of the Second Corps read the order and crumpled it savagely in his fist.

"They can't get reinforcements to us," he said. "Major Moore, go to the right at once; Captain Markoe, you and Captain Jones to the left. Tell every commander to prepare for withdrawal. It's going to be harder to get back to where we started than it was to come here."

He was right. From both flanks and from the forts along the railroad, batteries of guns were roaring and bellowing. Shot and shell seemed to fill the morning air. As the Confederates abandoned the works they had seized, the fire became withering.

Many of the retreating force fell before they could return to the old line of trenches. Clay stayed with Gordon, who did not leave the fort until the last of the infantry was on its way. Then, as dawn became full daylight, the racket of bombardment rose loudly to the right of the repulsed Second Corps.

"Trust old Ulysses S. Grant to know what to do in a case like this," Clay heard Colonel Douglas saying. "All our concentration of troops against Fort Stedman told him that the lines must be thinly held there at the west, and he's counterattacking."

"Our chance of getting through and striking the railroad was one in a hundred," mourned Captain Markoe.

Gordon overheard the captain. He turned around from where he stood with a surgeon plastering the wound on his upper arm.

"We had to take that one chance and hope it succeeded," he fairly roared out. "Don't stand there worrying because it failed—worry won't help. See to our lines, see if they're ready to withstand an assault, because it will be coming."

It was true. The great Federal host hammered the entire Confederate line below Petersburg all that day and far into the night. The Second Corps had lost heavily in its unsuccessful attack—more than three thousand in killed, wounded, and missing, Clay heard. But it faced the bombardment and the volleys of bullets stanchly, and gave back a fierce fire of its own. Elsewhere the Federals stormed and captured parts of the trenches, driving the outnumbered Southerners back to the second line of defense and taking hundreds of prisoners.

There followed days of striving, straining toil and battle. Clay seldom had a chance to pull off his boots when he lay down at night. The reduced infantry regiments held their defenses with the thinnest of lines; Clay saw men standing eight or ten feet apart in the ditches, ragged, weary, and hungry, but with eyes as bright as their cocked ready muskets. Clay rode constantly with orders and reports, sometimes creeping out under the storm of bullets to scout Federal movements, and he, too, went hungry. The greater part of his scanty ration of corn he gave to Cherokee, who carried him bravely.

On the night of March 31, the couriers of Second Corps headquarters gathered to eat sweet potatoes baked in the ashes, and swap news and rumors.

"Sherman has his whole army at Goldsboro in North Carolina, up near Raleigh, this minute," volunteered Jim Sloan.

"How far's that from here?" asked his companion beside the fire.

"About a hundred and twenty miles," estimated Jim. "Sherman might be heading up here to help Grant against us. At least he's not going over toward Clay's home in eastern North Carolina. I reckon you think that's a mercy, Clay."

"I wish Sherman wasn't going anywhere but back

to wherever he lived before the war," said Clay, thinking of Dr. Winstead at the Raleigh hospital.

"And Sheridan's driven the last of our troops out of the Shenandoah Valley, and he's brought over 13,000 cavalry," chimed in another. "I hear tell there's a movement of infantry along that railroad, to go west and join him. Maybe they're going to pinch off the Southside Railroad at last."

"Well, what can we do about it?" asked Jim. "If anybody has a suggestion, I'm ready."

"There's not much left to do but pray," spoke up Sergeant Drumm. "Pray for more strength and more courage—"

"Wouldn't that be praying all wrong?" Jim broke in. "Why don't you pray for more rations, Sergeant? We've got more courage in this army right now than we have any use for."

And he popped the last morsel of his baked potato into his hungry mouth.

Two days later Second Corps headquarters heard of a crushing Federal victory at Five Forks, just to the right of the Confederate line. The division of George E. Pickett, who at Gettysburg had led the great charge almost to victory, had been badly shattered, and Fitz Lee's cavalry had suffered. Even while officers and couriers digested this grave news, came more and worse. A bloody battle on the morning of April 2 had resulted in the driving in of the whole Confederate left. General A. P. Hill, commander of the Third

Corps, had been killed in action, and Robert E. Lee himself had been forced to abandon the headquarters where once Clay had spoken with him.

"Now what?" wondered the couriers.

The answer came at once from Gordon.

The Army of Northern Virginia had been ordered to abandon the defenses of Petersburg and Richmond, to try to escape from Grant and head south and west. Down there somewhere—nobody knew exactly where —was Johnston's army. The two forces would join and fight side by side.

"Fight?" Clay echoed the word when Drumm told him. "Fight Grant or fight Sherman?"

"Fight them both, I reckon," said the sergeant. "Buckner, just how did everything go wrong?"

"That's an easy one to answer," replied Clay bitterly. "We've fought our best, fought better than men ever fought; but there aren't enough of us."

"No," agreed Drumm. "And there never were enough of us, never once from the beginning."

Even as they spoke, the sound of battle rose. The Union troops were assailing the Second Corps infantry in the trenches.

❧ 12 ❦

Flight from Petersburg

The couriers sped in all directions with orders. These were bleakly terse and informative. The Second Corps would fight all that day, holding its line of breastworks at all hazards, to give Longstreet's First Corps and the broken remains of other commands a chance to draw away and begin their march to westward. Then, under cover of darkness, the Second Corps would fall back out of the trenches, march by way of a bridge across the Appomattox to east of Petersburg, and join the departing column above the river.

The first infantry officer to whom Clay handed these orders read them with a face that glowed suddenly with the hard light of pride.

"The Second Corps will be the rear guard," he said. "We'll hold the enemy off while the others get started out of Petersburg. Good old Second Corps! We've taken the rub and had the glory of all the hard jobs ever since we went marching ourselves flat-footed with old Stonewall Jackson."

It was a proud boast, felt Clay, but it was not a vain

one. He remembered a score of fierce fights in which the Second Corps had won its honors, not least gallant of which had been that desperate attempt to take and hold Fort Stedman a week before.

The common soldiers, too, were fiercely ready to fight that rear-guard action. Their spirits lifted with a welcome issue of rations, more bread and meat than they had seen for many days. Clay and Jim and the other couriers gobbled eagerly as they sped here and there on errands for Gordon's staff.

As the sun set, Clay watched the start of Gordon's long wagon train. There were strings of ambulances and supply carts, and then the artillery. Many of the heavy guns had to be abandoned for lack of horses to pull them. Bitterly mourning their pet pieces, the gun crews chopped the wheels to bits and drove spikes into the touchholes. At the front, the night was torn with fire and deafening din—a Federal assault, to which the infantry replied with measured volleys of musketry.

Finally, just before midnight, the last of the defenders climbed out of the works they had held so long, and formed on the road, to march away.

A few miles to the rear, the regiments tramped across a wooden bridge that spanned the Appomattox. Gordon reined in on the far side, Clay and Jim behind him, to watch until the last soldier was on the north bank. Then Gordon called to an officer of engineers.

"Set that bridge afire," he ordered harshly. "Get it blazing from end to end. I don't want a single board left on those piers."

The general watched, his head sunk between his shoulders. The glare of the bright flames showed his face locked in a frown.

"He doesn't look very glad to leave Petersburg," remarked Clay.

"He isn't glad," said Jim. "Didn't you hear? His wife is staying there, with their baby son. This won't be the sort of picnic excursion you can take ladies and babies on, not by a long shot."

"What will happen to them?"

"General Gordon's counting on good manners and kindness from the Yankees. He's confident that his family will be well treated."

"I think he's right," said Clay. "Maybe Colonel Tryon will be in Petersburg, looking after Mrs. Gordon."

They followed their general away in the night, behind the last regiment of the Second Corps.

It was a long march in the thick darkness. The hard-bitten infantrymen managed to go mile after mile, with only brief rests, well into the morning of Monday, April 3. Somewhere off to the south, below the Appomattox, they heard occasional scattered bursts of fire, but no sustained noise of battle.

"I think we've managed to get clear away from them," said Colonel Douglas to Clay as they rode beside the column. "Grant must be groping around after us right now, but he's lost touch. And, man for man, I don't think he can outwalk us any more than he can outfight us."

The march had been pointed toward Bevill's Bridge, to cross the Appomattox again and head southward; but word came back from the men ahead that the spring rains had flooded Bevill's Bridge. On they traveled that day, with a rest stop at noon, a chance to sprawl and eat the last of the rations they had saved from yesterday's generous issue. At night Gordon's brigades camped in trampled brush a good eighteen miles from where they had left the burning bridge on their departure from the trenches.

Clay saw the worn-out, hungry infantry stretched out almost in their own tracks, sleeping soundly. Only weary, sagging sentries were on their feet. But Clay and Cherokee had no rest. Gordon sent Clay with Captain Jones to make sure of a crossing upstream from the flooded span.

They found it some miles ahead, a stout wooden structure called Goode's Bridge. Most of the First Corps had found their way across and were camped beyond the south bank of the Appomattox, and more troops were arriving by night from the road that led northward to abandoned Richmond. Jones questioned some officers there, and seemed happy as he and Clay rode back.

"President Davis and his party made it safely away by train before we even began to retire," he said. "And this army has slipped away from Grant, too. From here we'll go on to Amelia Court House, just a few miles past Goode's Bridge. And General Lee has ordered trainloads of rations to roll down there and wait for us."

Gordon heard this news with grave pleasure. "I'm glad to hear about the rations," he said when Jones had finished. "I don't think there's a mouthful of cornbread or beef left in the whole Second Corps. Let the word be passed on to the men that we can count on a good meal not long after noon tomorrow. That will help them pick up their poor sore feet. Now, then, what does anybody know about the location of the enemy?"

"That's good news, too," replied Captain Jones. "Judging by all we hear from Fitz Lee's cavalry scouts, Grant's army is still back there around Petersburg, trying to find out what became of us. Marse Robert stole a good day's march on him."

"If we can keep that lead, Grant will never catch up," elaborated Gordon happily. "Not in time to cause any trouble, anyway. Only his cavalry can get to us fast enough, and we can take care of all the cavalry the North ever sent down. Once we're clear away from his fastest scouts, Grant will be forced to move slowly and send out patrols here and there to find which road we took."

"And which road do we take, General?" Jones made bold to ask.

"From Amelia Court House we'll undoubtedly push on down to Danville. There are supplies there. Beyond that point, there's North Carolina and Johnston's army." Gordon glanced up and saw Clay standing with

Cherokee's bridle in his hand. "I see you're listening to all this, Buckner."

"I'm sorry if I shouldn't listen, General," apologized Clay.

"No, no, it's all right. I need you with me, and Sloan, too. You're North Carolinians, and once we're in your home state I'll count on you-all to guide us to wherever Johnston will be waiting."

Clay loosened Cherokee's saddle girth and found a handful of straw to rub down his beloved horse's legs. Cherokee began to crop grass gratefully, and Clay was glad that he, at least, was a Confederate that had found rations. He himself did not spread his blankets, but lay down on his overcoat beside a fire of twigs which the couriers had made. Sergeant Drumm, Jim Sloan, and the others talked about the day's march and the prospects of future marches and battles.

"We sure enough aren't a big army any more," said Drumm. "I don't reckon we've got more than thirty-five thousand men on their feet. But Johnston must have near about as many as that, down there in Carolina. And they're a fighting crowd, too—they gave Sherman three days of right lively action at some place called Bentonville."

"What kind of fighters are Sherman's men?" asked Jim.

"Pretty good, from what I hear tell. After all, they've fought their way all the way from the Mississippi to the Georgia coast. But," and Drumm's fluffy-bearded young face looked thoughtful, "I just don't judge they're as hard a set to scuffle with as Grant's Army of the Potomac. At least, they don't shove Johnston as hard as Grant has shoved Lee."

"How many men has Sherman?" was Clay's question.

"I've heard some guesses about that. They run from sixty to ninety thousand. But," and Drumm's voice grew almost gay, "when we get there and join Johnston, we'll have an army of better than sixty thousand."

"Do tell!" cried another courier. "With that many, and less than that many, Marse Robert has swallowed bigger armies than Sherman's and spit 'em out again. Remember Chancellorsville? Remember the second Manassas?"

Jim glanced at Clay. "Old Wade Hampton's with Johnston, with his cavalry and the rest of the Iron Scouts. It'll be good to see them again."

"And we've got generals better than any that ever buckled on a sword," pointed out Clay, his own spirits rising. "Longstreet and Gordon, chiefs of division like Mahone and Grimes and Kershaw—"

"And in command of everything, Robert E. Lee," summed up Sergeant Drumm. "Gentlemen, hush! I wouldn't be in old Sherman's boots then, not if they were made of solid gold from cuff to toe."

They exulted, but they were too sleepy to talk further. They slept like logs on the hard earth, with the smoldering fire to keep them warm.

Before dawn, the army was awake and moving again. The news that there was food at Amelia Court House, and a promised halt for rest, made tired, starved men move cheerfully and well, even as Gordon had hoped. By midmorning, the last of the Second Corps rear guard had crossed Goode's Bridge. Riding to the head of his command, Gordon pointed them southward toward Amelia Court House.

"I know you didn't have any breakfast," he called out as he rode along the line, "but neither did I. And you and I are going to wait for our noon dinner. But it's just a few miles down there to where we'll stop, and I hope the rations will taste as good to you as they're going to taste to me."

Something like a cheer greeted these words, and the men slogged stubbornly on, while the sun grew high and gratefully warm. At least, no enemies were in sight, not even to the scouts along the eastward flank. The troops ahead were moving well, too. By mid-afternoon, Gordon ordered his men to fall out and make their camp north of the little town of Amelia Court House.

A staff officer rode up to where Gordon had dismounted and given Clay the reins of his horse.

"Where are you from?" Gordon demanded. "First Corps, eh? Glad to see you, sir. When do our rations arrive?"

"I don't know, General Gordon," was the melancholy reply.

"Don't know?" Gordon barked, and, "Don't know?" echoed half a dozen of his staff.

"Those trains didn't get to town, sir. I heard the

orders that came from General Lee for all the empty wagons to start out through the country to find what food might be left."

"We have to forage," Gordon said despairingly. "That means we're stuck here, tired out and starved, while those well-fed Yankees catch up with us."

"I'm afraid that's the truth of it, General," glumly agreed the rider from the First Corps.

Gordon gestured fiercely at his companions. "Douglas, Markoe, Jones! Go pass the word to the division and brigade commanders. Let foraging parties go out and get anything. Anything, mind you—a pig or a chicken or a handful of meal. Buckner, you and Sloan used to be Iron Scouts, you understand foraging. Mount, and go find any mouthful you can and bring it back."

Cherokee was tired from more than two weeks of daily cantering, but he responded to Clay's word. Jim rode with Clay to a farm on a nearby hill, then to other farms beyond, among groves and hollows. But the two riders knew before they asked what the answer would be.

That country had already been visited many times in past months by foraging details from both armies. Corncribs and barns and pens had been stripped bare. The farmers themselves were in want.

One thin, mild old man offered Clay a skinny piece of bacon that could not have weighed more than half a pound. Clay took it, with the best thanks he could speak, and the old man would not accept the greenback offered in payment. At another door, a sober-faced woman brought out a little home-woven basket with eight eggs in it.

"Take 'em along, youngster," she urged him. "No, I won't keep even one. If General Lee's going through here, them Yankees will be right along after him in a few hours, and I'd a heap rather let you have all my hen's eggs than any folks from up North that I never invited down here in the first place."

"The Yankees will take your hen," reminded Clay.

She smiled and shook her head. "Not that hen. I've got her in the stewpot now, and we'll eat her up before ary bluecoat comes knocking."

"What can I pay you, ma'am?"

"Just give me a smile, sonny. That's right. And when you all come back, chasing old Grant out of here, I'll be waiting. Maybe with more eggs for you all."

As Clay rode back with these small gleanings, Jim joined him with two loaves of light bread, the gift of another farm family that had just done its week's baking. Back in camp, Gordon's officers and couriers thronged around the bread, eggs, and bacon—more than a dozen hungry men.

"That looks like the breakfast we missed this morning," said Colonel Douglas. "How shall we divide it?"

"We won't divide it at all," decreed Gordon. "We'll just mix it up and parcel it out in equal shares. Drumm, you're a good cook as well as a good sergeant of couriers. Take charge and see how far you can stretch those things."

Drumm did so. One courier he set to slicing up the two loaves of bread, and another to frying the bacon in several skillets. He himself broke the eggs into a battered tin pan and whipped them vigorously with an old fork. Then he dipped the slices of bread one at a time into the beaten egg, and fried them in the bacon fat. Surprisingly and gratifyingly, there was a fair helping for every officer and man in the headquarters group.

"Gentlemen," announced Gordon, finishing his own share, "I venture to guess that this headquarters has eaten as well as any mess in the army. I wish that General Lee had been close enough to invite to supper with us."

The Army of Northern Virginia slept with near-empty stomachs that night. It woke breakfastless on April 5, and the wagons again sought supplies throughout the surrounding country and came back with almost nothing. After noon—dinnerless noon—the march began again, and the pursuing blue van of Grant's army was already in sight.

≥ 13 ≤

The Terrible March

As the Second Corps drew its rear regiments away from Amelia Court House, loud explosions sounded and clouds of smoke and dust arose.

"Shell fire," said Clay, staring over his shoulder.

"No," Colonel Douglas told him, "that's extra ammunition being blown up. We've been hoarding it all these four years of war, and now it has to be destroyed because we can't take it along with us and it mustn't fall into the hands of the enemy."

Only cavalry of the pursuing Union host was catching up, but it came in regiments and pressed close. Again and again the blue cavalry dismounted and opened fire like infantry. Gordon sent Clay to ride with an order for the division of General Bryan Grimes to deploy and fight.

"I want that cavalry stopped where it is," Gordon said. "I want it slowed down and kept from riding up on our flanks where it can do real damage."

Behind the main body, Grimes sent two of his brigades into line of battle. These sent volleys into the bluecoats and then fell back, while another line stood ready to fight a delaying action in its turn. The march went on without halt—four miles, five. Then another distant sound of crackling gunfire, this time from up ahead. Along came a courier, whipping his bony horse into a lather, to thrust a paper into Gordon's hands. Every hair of the general's dark beard bristled as he read.

"Grant came up while we were waiting there at Amelia Court House," he said tautly. "A big force of his cavalry managed to get ahead of us, below Jetersville, and cut off the railroad to Danville. We've got to march westward now."

"March how far?" asked Colonel Douglas.

"To Farmville. We can expect supplies—I hope it's true this time—at Farmville. General Lee telegraphed to Lynchburg for a train to be loaded and sent to us along the Southside Railroad. Now, how far is it from here to Farmville?"

Douglas pulled a map from his saddlebag. He and Gordon walked their horses side by side to look at it. Clay saw Gordon moving his long forefinger to trace the way.

"I make it twenty miles or more, sir," said Douglas. "Say twenty-three."

"Twenty-three miles," repeated Gordon. "Every step of it without food for these men, and maybe with fighting. We'll have to march the rest of today and all night."

"Can we do it, General?" asked Douglas. "Can the troops do it?"

"They must!" Gordon barked at him. "We have to march or die. This is the hardest marching order I've ever received since the day I set foot on the banks of Bull Run four years ago. But we have to do it."

Turning in his saddle, he raised his voice to speak to the others of the staff.

"Take these marching orders to the division commanders, and tell them to pass them on to their brigade commanders," he directed. "Let them use their own judgment about informing the men. I myself hate to do it. All I can say is, the Army of Northern Virginia is being asked to do the fastest, cruelest marching it ever did. But if we can pull ahead of the Yankees, if we can get to Farmville and rest and eat there, we'll be ourselves again."

So strongly did his deep voice ring that the others nodded as though they believed and agreed. The command went out to change the line of march.

But it was a nightmare of a journey. Grimes's men had driven back the first threatening cavalry and there was no pressing call to battle, but nothing else might comfort the Confederates. As the column staggered on into the evening, Gordon sent Clay to ride along the flank for news of how the men endured.

"We'll make it," a lean, thicket-bearded captain answered Clay's question. "Right now I figure we're outmarching those Yankees. It's like that old fable about how the rabbit outran the dog—the dog was running for his dinner, but the rabbit was running for his life."

"I'm runnin' for my dinner too, Cap'n," a marching soldier was able to joke. "And for the dinner I missed today and the dinner I missed yesterday. I sure enough hope there's three dinners a-waitin' for me up ahead."

As Clay neared the head of the Second Corps column, he saw two riders sitting their horses at the side of the road. Approaching in the dimness, he wondered at the cleanness of their gray uniforms, the fine condition of their glossy mounts. He, too, reined in and waited at a little distance. Minutes later, Sergeant Drumm and Jim Sloan caught up with him.

"Help me decide on two mighty well-fed fellows up yonder," said Clay, and the three advanced together. "Look," said Clay. "They're counting our files, seeing how many men we have left."

"They're spies," declared Drumm.

"That's what I think," said Clay. "Pull out and come up behind them. I'll go tell them they've been arrested."

Drawing his pistol, he urged the tired Cherokee to a trot. "You're under arrest," he called to the two men as he came near.

They looked toward him. A scrap of moon shone down. "What do you mean?" demanded the taller of the pair. "You're talking to a superior officer, my boy. I'm a lieutenant of Fitzhugh Lee's cavalry."

"I'm talking for your superior officer," replied Clay, "General Gordon. Come along with me."

"Do as he says," seconded Jim from behind them.

"You're going to be sorry about this," promised the tall lieutenant.

Clay looked at him more closely. There was something familiar about that voice, but the night was too dark to see the face under the low-drawn hat. Back toward the rear they herded the two men. As they did so, the column halted for a rest. They found Gordon and his staff at the roadside, and one of the officers had lighted a fire. At Clay's word, the two prisoners dismounted.

"General Gordon," said the lieutenant, "this man of yours is making a mistake. He thinks we're spies."

"And are you?" asked Gordon.

"Certainly not, General. We're coming back from sick leave, trying to find our way to General Fitzhugh Lee's cavalry." He held out a paper. "Here's my pass. Show him yours, Corporal."

They moved close to the fire. Clay saw their faces in the light.

"I say they're Federal spies, General," he called out at once. "They took me prisoner this last January." He stepped close to the lieutenant. "Hello, Dave Wagner. Do you remember me? You took me to City Point. And this is your partner, Ike Murray."

"You must be dreaming," said the shorter man. "I never heard of any Ike Murray. My name's on that pass."

Gordon was studying the papers. "These are signed by Fitz Lee himself, Buckner."

"Forgeries," said Clay. "We always carried forged passes in the Iron Scouts."

"But I know Fitz Lee's handwriting," Gordon argued.

"Then they captured passes from some of our cavalry," insisted Clay. "I tell you, sir, I know them both. They're Jessie Scouts of the Union Army, dressed in Confederate uniforms. We ought to search them."

"I agree," said Wagner mockingly. "When this imaginative young soldier is convinced of his mistake, General Gordon, I ask that he be arrested and tried by court-martial."

The two men pulled off their jackets. Clay searched every pocket, fingered every seam. Jim looked in the pockets of their trousers and made them open their shirts.

"Finding anything, boys?" jeered Murray.

"Take off your boots," Clay ordered him.

"Must we?" sighed Wagner.

"Yes," said Gordon. "You must."

Wagner sat down by the fire and tugged off one high boot, then the other. Clay felt inside them. His hand found a slit in the lining of the right boot, and he poked his fingers into it.

"I've found a paper," he announced.

Wagner sprang to his feet, but Jim Sloan leveled a pistol. "Sit down again," he said, and Wagner shrugged, smiled, and obeyed.

Clay handed the paper to Gordon, who scowled as he read it. Then he faced the prisoners.

"This is a message from General Grant to General Ord," he said. "What have you two to say?"

"Ah," said Wagner, suddenly smiling, "all I can say

is that this young chap—I remember him well, he was one of the Iron Scouts—he's right about us."

"You know your fate," said Gordon. "Under the laws of war, you've forfeited your lives by wearing Confederate uniform. I can have you shot by sunrise tomorrow."

Wagner looked at Murray. Neither of them flinched.

"General, we understand that," said Wagner in a steady voice. "We knew when we went into the Jessie Scouts that we were taking our lives in our hands. We knew that we could be shot if we were captured. But this war won't last much longer. It won't do you any good to have us killed."

"Put on your boots again," Gordon told him. "Sloan, turn these men over to the prisoner detail, and tell the guards to watch them with special vigilance."

The staff officers and the couriers watched the two men being marched away. Gordon smiled.

"I don't intend to have them shot," he said. "But this captured order must go at once to General Lee. Grant has told Ord to move as fast as possible to cut us off at Appomattox Court House."

"Appomattox Court House!" echoed Clay.

Gordon looked at him quizzically. "What's the matter, Buckner?"

"My blood just froze, sir," said Clay.

In his mind was a vision of Lark Winstead as he had seen her last, and he could hear her voice, confident that she would be safe at Appomattox Court House from the dreadful approach of war.

Dawn came, and no breakfast. Instead came Federals, first a rushing cloud of cavalry, then infantry skirmishers, then solid columns of troops.

Hungry, outnumbered, tottering from day after day of tramping the roads, Gordon's men fought. The wagons ahead of them were stuck in the mud of an overflowing stream—Sayler's Creek was its name, someone said—and Clay and other couriers sprang from their horses to help shove wagon after wagon across to dry ground, while desperately the muskets and cannon barked and boomed. The fight rolled almost to the creekside where the wagons were bogged, but Gordon himself rode to the front, thundering an order for a charge that drove back the Federals. Advance and withdrawal followed each other, hour after hour. More bombardment burst out to the south. The rest of Lee's army was fighting too.

"Buckner!" Clay heard Gordon yelling his name. "Get on your horse and ride there to the right. Find General Lee, give him this report. I won't ask him for help, he won't have any to spare me. I'm just saying that we'll do our best to hold on and cover these wagons. I want his directions as to which way to move."

Clay rode as fast as Cherokee's weary legs could go. He found another battle going on. Even as he arrived, he saw Confederate infantry falling back from the firing line. Some of the men ran in disorder.

"Why are you running?" Clay shouted at one.

"Because I can't fly!"

"Where's General Lee?" Clay asked an officer, who

pointed beyond. Clay rode toward the gray man on the gray horse, just as Lee stooped from his saddle to catch a flag from the hand of a wounded soldier. Lee gathered up his reins as though to ride forward into the fight.

"No!" fairly screamed another horseman, a gnarled little man with a great bush of beard, like a gnome in uniform. "No, General!" said the bearded man. "Here are troops ready to do their duty—"

It was General Mahone. He took the flag from Lee's hand. Lee turned and gazed as another rank of infantry, dirty and skinny and ragged, ran gamely forward.

"Yes," said Lee, "there are some true men left." He pointed to the advancing Federals. "General, will you please keep those people back?"

Mahone waved the flag over his head and led the countercharge.

Among a spatter of whizzing bullets, Clay rode to Lee's side and handed him Gordon's message. Lee glanced at it, then turned to look at Clay.

"Say to General Gordon that he must withdraw as best he can, protecting the wagon train," Lee said. "He must go northward, to High Bridge across the Appomattox. But you were in danger, young man, riding through these bullets. You should have come around the hill yonder, to be under cover."

"General Lee, I'd be ashamed to do that when you're exposed here," said Clay.

"It's my duty to be here," said Lee, more sternly.

"You're riding with important messages. Go back the way I told you, sir."

Obediently Clay rode back to the shelter of the hill and made his roundabout way to Gordon in the late afternoon. The Second Corps had managed to beat off its pursuers, and followed the wagons toward High Bridge. But from Drumm, Clay heard that terrible losses had been sustained; seventeen hundred of the Second Corps were killed, wounded, or captured.

"At least we hurt the Yankees right smartly, too," said Drumm. "They don't seem to be hurrying to follow us up. By the way, General Gordon is making you a present."

"What kind of present?" asked Clay.

"Yonder it is, with Jim Sloan."

Jim rode a fine horse with a Federal saddle cloth, and led another.

"Gordon won't shoot those two spies you caught, but he's making them walk on foot with the other prisoners," said Drumm. "And he thinks you and Sloan deserve the horses you took from them."

Clay quickly changed from Cherokee to the captured horse.

"Good idea to rest Cherokee," approved Drumm. "When he's fresh he's the best horse in all this Second Corps, and you may need him in top shape for some special duty."

"Once across High Bridge, and we're close to Farmville," added Jim Sloan. "There's food there—lots of food."

❧ 14 ❧
Barricade of Fire

As the Southerners toiled along, news ran the length of the column of what that bitter fight had cost them. The casualties had amounted to more than seven thousand, and perhaps sixteen thousand men left in the ranks were still able to fight. Whole regiments, even divisions, had been wiped out. Some of the best generals had been captured by the Federals. Among these were Ewell, Kershaw, and the commanding general's son Custis Lee.

The wounded who could walk tried to keep up. Those who could not walk had to be left for the advancing Federals to find, perhaps to help. Riding his captured horse to rest Cherokee, Clay was busy here and there carrying messages and seeing that the various units kept contact. He saw many men without blankets, without haversacks, without muskets. They had thrown away these things, trying desperately to stay with Lee's retreat.

Even so, every mile of the march saw men dropping out, too utterly exhausted to keep up. No one had

anything to eat, except here and there a meager handful of shelled corn from the feed of the horses and
mules.

"We've lost men and guns," said a staff officer, "but
our worst loss was time. We had to slow up at Amelia
Court House, and we had to slow up again to fight
at Sayler's Creek. That let the enemy infantry catch
up. They're right behind us now."

"Strong, well-fed infantry," added Clay.

"Correct. The Army of Northern Virginia has done
its greatest march these last four days, and most of it
we've done starving. I know that we won't be able to
march another day without rations."

They crossed the Appomattox at High Bridge. Clay
noticed that the river was narrow and shallow here
so close to its headwaters. Night fell, chilly and gloomy,
as the famished, bone-weary soldiers staggered a few
miles on and camped on either side of the road near
Farmville. A few lights shone in town, and there was
talk of waiting food; but the infantry slept where it
had halted, too tired to feel hunger. And in the
morning, quartermasters brought wagons laden with
rations.

Clay heard the awakening soldiers cheer joyously,
and he himself charged those wagons as he might have
charged an enemy. Swiftly the drivers rolled barrels
to the ground, set them up, and ripped out the heads
with hatchets. Other men unloaded sacks of meal and
gashed them open with knives. The soldiers pressed
close around, while quartermaster sergeants dealt out

big pieces of smoked pork from the barrels and scooped rich, coarse meal into pans, bags, and the crowns of hats.

Clay found himself provided with at least six pounds of meat and a good two quarts of meal, which he tied up in a blue scarf long ago captured from the Federals. Balancing these prizes carefully on his saddle, he rode in search of Jim and found him also laden with rations. Even as they congratulated each other, Sergeant Drumm called to them.

"Come over here to this wagon," he yelled. "They're giving out molasses."

Jim and Clay produced pint mugs and drew them full of the thick sweet liquid. Then all three returned to the bivouac fire of the couriers. Their other comrades had found water to make dough for corn pone, and were frying strips of pork. Everybody munched with frantic appetite, while more pone and meat cooked on the fire.

"I wish I had appetite enough to eat forever," sighed a happy courier as he wiped the last trickle of molasses from his cup with a crusty piece of corn bread. "What will we do with the rest of that stuff in the pans? I couldn't swallow another mouthful."

"We'll carry that along to eat for dinner," Drumm informed him.

Barely had they bundled up the cooked rations when shots rang out on the road they had traveled. The Federals were coming again.

"Let 'em come!" roared out the courier who had

eaten so heartily. "I've had a champion breakfast; I'll fight like a tiger!"

Many had not had the chance to eat so well, and had to go into action still chewing. Gordon's rear division counterattacked, and the pursuit slowed up again. Men of the First Corps moved in to take the brunt of the assault, throwing earth up for defenses. Gordon drew his regiments out of the fight and moved them through some woods to protect the flank of the wagon train. The army was moving northward.

"Aren't we heading the wrong way to find Joe Johnston?" demanded Jim as the couriers rode after Gordon.

"The longest way around is the shortest way home," said Captain Jones. "Those Yanks moved to our left while we were fighting this morning, and they've put themselves between us and Danville. We'll follow the Lynchburg Road and try to turn south further on."

Clay heard this news with a calm that surprised him. He was dully weary with riding, scouting, fighting, and hoping. It seemed as though the march had lasted forever.

Now the Second Corps had moved to the front, ahead of the wagons and the artillery train, while the First Corps, with stout James Longstreet in command, covered the rear. The morning was warm after the chilly night, and the men in ranks seemed to grow more cheerful. Once or twice Clay heard snatches of a song he knew:

"On the plains of Manassas the Yankees we met,
 And we gave them a whipping they'll never forget—"

"I remember about that," said Jim Sloan heavily, "but it seems a hundred years since we fought at Manassas."

"It seems a hundred years since we fought at Petersburg," rejoined Clay.

"Both you boys are carrying your age well, then," Drumm tried to joke. "Neither one of you looks a day older than eighty-five."

Their objective was New Store, a twenty-mile march. They plodded northward, then westward, and constantly the pursuers were in view—cavalry riding across the fields to the south of them and infantry pressing from behind. But Longstreet did not have to fight such bitter rear-guard actions as had Gordon, and there were only occasional spatters of gunfire.

Still men dropped out of ranks. Clay and the others tried to urge them to keep going.

"I'm through going anywhere," panted one soldier, lying flat among bushes. "If I could move one foot ahead of the other, I'd keep marching; but I can't."

Wagons, too, broke down, and horses collapsed in their harness. The track of Lee's army could be followed by the string of such wreckage, animate and inanimate.

They reached New Store at last. It was neither new nor a store, but a simple crossing of two trampled roads, and a tumble-down hutlike building long ago abandoned by whoever had occupied it. Again came the welcome order to fall out, and there was hasty gobbling of rations brought from the issue outside Farmville, then drugged slumber on the hard ground. At one o'clock in the morning of April 8, Gordon waked his staff and his commanders. The army pushed on under the bright light of a moon nearly at the full.

"Which way are we heading?" Clay heard a soldier ask.

"Lynchburg, from what I hear," answered another.

"That's mighty good talk! I've been in Lynchburg, and there's mountains like saw teeth all around. We could stand off all the Yankees in the world if we get there."

"How far to Lynchburg, Sarge?"

"I can't say, boys. Maybe ten miles, maybe thirty. Keep your feet moving and we'll get there all the sooner."

Again the morning was bright, and some spirit of cheer and confidence ran through the worn-out ranks. Nobody was shooting at the Army of Northern Virginia today. Clay tried to be optimistic at heart. After all, Lee had twice marched entirely away from Grant, and only bad luck had slowed his troops down until Grant could catch up each time. Maybe this third time was the charm. Maybe they had escaped again, and permanently.

Late in the afternoon, orders were passed from regiment to regiment to halt and fall out on a long, gentle slope among sparse trees. Men moved with listless feet to make camp, then sat down and searched out the odds and ends of food that remained. At the foot of the slope crawled a narrow stream—a branch of the Appomattox. Beyond, at a distance of two or three miles, the roofs of a small settlement showed.

Clay dismounted from his new horse and tied it beside Cherokee under a young oak that sprouted its spring tassels. Near him, Captain Jones was unsaddling.

"What's the name of the town yonder, sir?" Clay inquired.

"That little place? Appomattox Court House."

Clay spun as though the wind had whipped him around, and gazed at the roofs again. Involuntarily he took half a dozen steps down the slope.

"No visiting, Buckner," said Jones quickly. "General Gordon wants every man in his place tonight and accounted for, in case we have to fight or move on an instant's notice."

"But I know someone at Appomattox Court House," said Clay.

"Sorry, this is no time for social calls."

The other couriers unsaddled. Guns rolled by, drawn by stumbling and broken-down teams, to cross the river below. Down went the sun, but the moon was high, touching all the slope with pale light. Campfires burned here and there. Clay sat by the two horses as they chewed dried grass he had gathered for them, and looked at the lights in the houses beyond the river.

Jim came and sat beside him. "Look," said Jim pointing. "There at the west, where the sun set."

"Just the last of the sun's glow," suggested Clay.

"No, because it's there to the south, too. And behind us."

Clay looked around the horizon. A dim rosiness hung three-quarters of the way around it, where night sky and black distance came together.

"Those are campfires," said Jim. "Hundreds and hundreds."

"The enemy." Again Clay looked westward. "They're across our way ahead, and on our flank and behind us. The only way out will be to the north."

Drumm came toward them. "Buckner? Is that you? Yes, and Sloan. General Gordon wants you both."

Rising, they made their way toward the fire that marked the command post of the Second Corps. Gordon stood apart from his officers. He nodded as the two couriers stopped before him and saluted.

"Have you eaten?" he asked.

"A little, sir," replied Clay for them both.

"Do you feel like taking a ride? No, I won't ask that, because I know you're both nearly worn out. But are you able to ride tonight?"

"Yes, sir," replied Jim.

"I'm glad to hear you say so. Because you're riding, and the fate of this army will ride with you." Gordon pointed to the western horizon. "You can see these enemy campfires across our way to Lynchburg."

"We were just talking about them, General," Clay said. "They've closed in everywhere but at the north."

"North is the direction I'm sending you. There's another man here, who's been in this part of Virginia. He's an old friend of yours, I think." He looked toward the officers on the other side of the fire. "Where's Dulin?"

"He's just arrived," came back Captain Markoe's voice, and a familiar figure approached. Clay and Jim quickly shook hands with their old comrade.

"Dulin's been with the cavalry, but I asked for him because you three have worked well together in the past," said Gordon. "Attention to orders: You'll ride out of camp, find your way around whatever force is in front of us to the west, and get behind it. Those Yankees have just arrived, and they won't be all over the country there. Back there somewhere—you'll have to find the place yourselves—is a road leading to the main Lynchburg road. They come together where there's a creek and a bridge across at that point. Some home guards from Lynchburg are stationed there. You must find the bridge and make sure it's passable, because the army will need it tomorrow."

"What will happen, General?" asked Jim.

"We don't think there's too strong a force in front of us. We'll cut our way through and make for Lynchburg. The Second Corps," and Gordon spoke with warm pride, "will open the attack. We have maybe eighteen hundred muskets to throw into the fight, but they're the flower of the army. All the weak souls have dropped away."

"And when do we advance?" Clay ventured to ask.

"As soon as there's light enough to see the enemy by. Once we've broken the enemy lines, we'll come through fast. We want that bridge ready to take our guns and wagons over, and we'll destroy it when we're all beyond it. The bridge is your responsibility. Now," Gordon wound up, "I'll let you choose which of you will command."

"Clay Buckner."

Both Jim Sloan and Bob Dulin said it in the same breath. Clay stared from one to the other, and Gordon laughed at him.

"Buckner, you're in charge by the vote of your comrades. You others will obey him in all things, as you'd obey Robert E. Lee himself. Any questions?"

"No, sir," said Clay, and, "No, sir," repeated the other two.

"Then start, and good luck to you."

He shook the hand of each in turn. Quickly Clay led them back to where the horses waited.

⩺ 15 ⩹
Moon over Appomattox

Clay put a saddle on Cherokee, who had rested ever since the battle of Sayler's Creek. Jim, too, had a fresh horse. From its scabbard Clay drew the breech-loading carbine and put it in Bob Dulin's hands.

"You admired that once, and you can have it now," he said. "Here, take this handful of cartridges."

"I'm still a few short of my hundred dead Yankees," said Bob grimly.

"Maybe we'll have to complete your total on this trip, but I hope we won't run into the need," Clay told him. "All right, let's mount and get out of here."

Quickly they rode from the camp. The moon showed them a narrow winding path to northward, and Clay moved up to take the lead. All three kept looking to the left, where the fires of the Union troops blazed in the distance.

Their horses were Iron Scout veterans like themselves, moving with sure confidence and knowledge in the moonlight. They had traveled two miles when Clay flung his arm up above his head and reined in. His friends came up on either side.

"Look," said Clay. "Those campfire reflections that showed to the west of the Second Corps camp are in the south now. None of them to the west of where we are."

"They'll have sent some pickets up this far," was Bob Dulin's guess.

"I know that. And see here, this little trail curves off westward. It's headed that way to join the main road leading north out of Appomattox Court House."

"The Bent Creek Road," contributed Jim. "I heard the name in camp."

"All right, their picket post probably will be where this trail joins the Bent Creek Road. They won't be looking for us to do any night march except along some kind of path. So we'll leave the trail right here, go a mile north, and try to slide past them there."

"Slide past to where?" Bob asked him.

"To the Lynchburg Road going west," replied Clay. "Our bridge is supposed to be on that road. In other words, three miles back south from where we are, and to the rear of whatever Federals are across the army's path." Clay looked at Bob, then at Jim. "Now, boys, you picked me to lead. I didn't ask for it, but here's my first order."

"Fire away, Lieutenant General Buckner," granted Jim.

"I'll keep on in the lead. You two come side by side, far enough apart for what might be the two flankers of a patrol, and watch to right and left. We haven't got a fourth man for a getaway rider, and anyway a getaway man wouldn't help if the rest of us got eaten up. Understand?"

"Right clearly," said Bob. He cradled the carbine across his saddle.

"And if we do run into Yankees, I'll tell them we're Jessie Scouts, like that pair of men Jim and I caught three nights ago. And I'll try not to let them ask the questions; I'll ask questions of my own—who are they, where's headquarters, are they ready to stop a quick move of the Confederates to southward. We'll act as if we're bringing orders from the rear. If I can't convince them, you two open fire, and we'll try to ride on through and get away."

"Right," agreed Jim.

"Just give me a chance to start shooting," said Bob Dulin darkly.

"Then here we go. Watch left and right, and watch me, too, for signals. If I have to raise my voice, I'll hoot like an owl—once to stop, twice for you to come ahead. Here we go."

Again he led off. They departed to the right of the little path, and moved slowly across a field that had been recently plowed. There was a narrow belt of trees beyond, then more open country. No adventures for a full mile. Then Clay gestured wide-armed for the party to turn westward, and set Cherokee's head for a ride around the flank. Again there was no sign of friend or enemy; but when he approached the Bent

Creek Road, a pale ribbon of dust in the moonlight, he hooted for a halt and dismounted, to steal forward, peer, and listen. Two more hoots, and he led them across the road and beyond.

The distant red glow of the campfires was dim to the south, as though a considerable distance away. On traveled the three scouts, and on. Clay judged that they had ridden fully five miles west when they saw trees ahead, a thick dark growth that seemed to mark a watercourse. He halted Cherokee and hooted twice. Up trotted Jim and Bob.

"I reckon that's our creek yonder," said Clay, pointing. "Hold the horses, Jim, and Bob and I will go make sure. Come along when you hear two hoots."

Bob Dulin held the carbine at the ready as Clay and he moved forward into the night. When they approached the trees, they could hear the sound of moving water. They stole among the trunks to the very brink. Moonlight filtered between the branches to show that it was not a wide creek, but Clay judged that it ran deep, among the shadows. Bob went scouting upstream for twenty or thirty yards, then came back.

"There's a way through the trees up there," he said in an undertone. "Looks like a ford."

Clay followed him, knelt down, and studied the water. It widened, and a patch extended beyond. Clay raised his voice in two hootlike cries.

"Wait here while Jim fetches the horses," he whispered. "I'll wade across and watch out on the far side while you all come through."

Bob faced back toward the east, and Clay crossed the creek. The bottom was firm beneath him, and the depth at the middle was no more than to his knees. On the west bank, he could see into more open country, quiet and dreamy in the moonlight. When Jim and Bob arrived with the horses, Clay climbed the tallest tree he could find.

From its topmost branches he could see the glow of fires to the southwest, a great constellation of them on the slope where they had left Gordon, and a smaller redness opposite, also south and west from where he had climbed. If Federals were there, they were not in tremendous force. Maybe the army could fight its way through. If any army could do that, Lee's army could. Sliding back down to earth, Clay mounted Cherokee again.

"Come on," he ordered, and rode forward again to the leader's position.

Now they moved to the south, beyond the stream. A road ran along its bank part of the way, but wisely they avoided it, staying to westward.

What time was it? Clay glanced up at the stars, the moon. It was getting late, he decided, eleven o'clock or so. But if they didn't have bad luck they'd come to the bridge by midnight.

He was nervous in his exercise of command on so important a mission. Twice he hooted the signal for a halt, and he and his friends scouted back to the creekside. Each time Clay climbed a tree to observe. The second time, he saw that they had returned southward to a point well behind the fires built by the Union troops. He could see single points of light but he could make out no bodies of troops in the distance. He and his two companions had come close to the road where the bridge should be found and examined for the state of its repair and its value to the retreating Army of Northern Virginia.

Jim took the point position after that, rode to the front, and hooted twice. The others came up to him. There, broad and straight, stretched the way to Lynchburg, with no sign of movement upon it.

"How far to safety from here?" asked Jim.

"I figure we're a good five miles west of where we started," said Clay. "And the distance to Lynchburg from there was maybe twenty miles. If the boys can fight their way this far, probably they're safe. We can stave off the enemy all the way to the mountains around Lynchburg."

The three young soldiers grinned at each other in the light of the moon, as though the escape of the army had been already accomplished. Then Clay pointed eastward once again.

"Let's move along to the south of this road, and slowly," he said. "I'll go first, you two in single file behind. Keep a lookout for the bridge, and let's be careful in coming up to it. There's supposed to be a detail of home guards, and they'll be nervous. Maybe they'll shoot at us before we can tell them we're friends."

They walked their horses along half a mile, then Clay put up his arm for a halt.

"Trees ahead," he said. "And I hear voices."

The night breeze brought the voices, deep and loud.

"What are those home guards doing, making a racket like that?" wondered Bob Dulin scornfully.

"We'll have to calm them down," suggested Clay. "Leave the horses here. Let's just hang their bridles to this bush, so if we come back in a hurry we can jump on and ride without stopping to untie. Now, Jim, Bob, we'll move forward on foot."

They could see the trees that marked the crossing of the creek at right angles to the road. Stealing along at a crouch, they heard the voices grow louder and louder. A fire burned among the trees. Beside it a man laughed, rather fiercely. Clay motioned for his party to drop down and approach on hands and knees. They reached the trees downstream, and slipped toward the firelight under cover.

"I'm sorry for you people," Clay heard the good-humored declaration. "You aren't really Rebel soldiers, nobody we want to kill or take prisoner."

And Clay knew the speaker. It was Colonel Tryon.

He drew his revolver. Bob had the carbine to the fore. Jim poised his musket. Closer they edged.

Past a tree they could see the fire, a small one, burning at the western end of the sturdy bridge of logs with low railings. A little knot of men in shabby gray stood there, and several other men in dark uniforms were gathered around them, leaning on rifles. In the full light of the fire Clay saw Tryon, his hat off and in his right hand, a smile on his side-whiskered face.

"Suppose we make a bargain with you," he was

offering. "You home guards take those axes and rip this bridge out by the roots. Then—and this is a promise—you can all go back to Lynchburg, or wherever you live, and forget about playing soldier. The war's going to be over with—in a few hours, anyway."

"Hear that?" muttered Jim.

"They've got those home guards and they're going to destroy the bridge," Bob whispered grimly.

"Not yet, they won't," said Clay.

He sprang upright. "Charge them!" he yelled at the top of his lungs.

Forward he rushed, Bob and Jim with him. All three of them howled the Rebel yell as though they were the advance of a hundred attacking Southern troops.

One of Tryon's men tried to bring up his rifle, but Clay was upon him and knocked him down with the barrel of his revolver. Half a dozen others were so amazed that they only stood and babbled.

"Hold up your hands!" roared Jim Sloan.

They dropped their weapons. One tried to flee, but Bob's carbine barked in the night. The fellow spun around as he reached the bridge, and fell face downward upon its rough brown planks.

Tryon had dropped his hat to grab for his own pistol, but Clay had caught Tryon's elbow and leveled his own weapon. "Don't move," he barked. "You're the last man in the Union army I want to shoot, but—"

With his other hand he possessed himself of the revolver at Tryon's waist. "Round up those others," he called to Jim and Bob. "Have they all flung down their guns? Grab them up, you home guards. Jim, hustle across the bridge and see if this is all the Yankees there are around here."

Tryon had been staring in utter blank amazement. Now he was able to smile again. His teeth flashed in the firelight.

"Well," he said, "so it's Clay Buckner. Clay, I might have foreseen that something like this would happen."

"Dare to move," Bob was growling at the other captured Federals. "Just dare. My trigger finger never itched worse during this whole long war."

The released home guards were seven in number. They had caught up weapons and surrounded their late captors. One of them, wearing a sergeant's stripes on his homemade jacket, saluted as though Clay were an officer.

"This party sneaked up on us while we were busy fixing the bridge up," he said apologetically. "We didn't even know they were there. I reckon we never learned how to watch out for surprises."

"Things are all right now," Clay told him. "Send one of your men back along the road to bring up our horses. Where's Jim? Any sign of more trouble to the east, Jim?"

"Nary whisper of it," said Jim, returning. "Just these Yankees' horses, tied to the bridge rail on the other side."

He knelt beside the man Bob had shot. "This poor

lad looks done for. No, he's wounded. I hear him groaning."

"See what you can do for him," said Clay.

"Let me," offered Tryon, and bent down over the fallen figure. "Where are you hit, Chadwick?"

"Body wound," wheezed the man.

"Did you say Chadwick?" demanded Clay. "The expert tracker that nearly led you after me to Iron Scout headquarters?"

"That's right, he's one of this bunch of headquarters scouts I brought out with me." Tryon had squatted down and carefully lifted Chadwick's head. "Stir up that fire so we can see."

Jim, Tryon, and Clay carried Chadwick nearer to the light. Bob Dulin came close. He stooped to look.

"Yank!" he said. "Are you hurt badly, Yank?"

"Mighty badly, it seems," answered Tryon for Chadwick.

"Then let's do something for him." Bob flung aside the carbine and tore Chadwick's blouse open. "Look at all that blood!"

Bob stared sickly at the damage his shot had done. "Hasn't anybody got any bandages?" he demanded. "Some of you home guards ought to have fetched handkerchiefs from Lynchburg."

"Let me look," said one of the guardsmen, a high-voiced boy. "My father's a doctor."

He had flung off his gray blouse and was stripping off his white shirt. Quickly he tore it up. He and Tryon wadded compresses against the two mouths of the wound on Chadwick's chest and back, and then bound more pieces of the shirt firmly around the body. Bob sat on his heels, looking on in helpless concern. Another guardsman offered a canteen. Bob fairly snatched it from his hand and held it to Chadwick's lips.

"You're named Chadwick, isn't that right?" he said. "Do you feel any better, Chadwick?"

Chadwick drank, and smiled. "A little bit better," he said. "Thanks, Johnny."

"Listen, you doctor's boy," said Bob to the one who was helping with the bandages, "how bad off is he?"

"I don't know, but I think that bullet may have scraped his lung," was the reply. "He needs a real surgeon, not a jackleg like me, and he ought to have the best of care."

"We'll get it," vowed Bob. "Listen, I never shot a Yank so close before, I never saw how one looked when he was hit. Take it easy, Chadwick. We'll get you a surgeon. We'll pull you through."

"Now," said Clay, "I want two of the steadiest of you guardsmen to watch over these prisoners. The rest of you grab up those axes and get back to work on the bridge. Robert E. Lee's whole army, horse, foot, and artillery, is going to cross here tomorrow morning."

≫ 16 ≪
Silence

Four of the home guards began to drag hewn timbers to the bridge and fit them into place over worn and splintered stretches of the floor. The other two, frowning importantly, watched the prisoners. Clay walked to the bridge and peered through the gloom to investigate its condition. Beyond, the horses of Tryon's party stood patiently. Tryon sauntered along with Clay, chatting in friendly fashion.

"You're wasting your time and the effort these men are making," he said. "I brought my little patrol this far behind our own camps to see what the road was like. When we don't come back, there'll be a bigger force sent out to find us."

"How close are your camps?" asked Clay.

"Oh, come now, Clay," laughed Tryon. "If I had you prisoner and asked you that sort of question about your army, you'd never answer it."

They returned across the bridge. The man who had been sent for the three horses arrived from the west.

"Jim," said Clay, "ride across the bridge and see how

close you can get to the rear of the enemy positions."

"And let that other man go to work on the bridge," pleaded Bob Dulin. "Send back the doctor's boy to look after Chadwick here; he acts mighty poorly."

The substitution was made. Bob neither guarded prisoners nor watched for the possible approach of other Federals. He stood gazing at Chadwick with a sort of embarrassed concern.

"He seems like a right nice fellow," said Bob to Clay. "Told me he doesn't hold it against me, my plugging him. Calls it the fortunes of war. I sure enough hope he pulls through all right."

"I hope so, too," agreed Clay honestly, and decided to say nothing about Bob's four-year ambition to shoot one hundred enemies. "Stir up the fire to keep him warm."

"And let me get that bedding roll off my saddle." Bob unstrapped and unrolled it, and quickly huddled a blanket around Chadwick. "There," he said. "That ought to make you feel some better."

"A lot better," said Chadwick, feebly but cheerfully.

"I'm glad to hear it." Kneeling, Bob wiped Chadwick's face with a cloth. "Here, you other Yanks, do any of you have some coffee in your saddlebags? Let's brew some of it for Chadwick; it might give him strength."

Jim came riding back to report that he had located the rear of the Federals three miles eastward. They were sleeping around their fires on both sides of the road. All sentries were observing alertly toward the Confederate lines.

The home guard sergeant approached Clay. "This bridge is as solid as any men can fix it tonight," he said proudly. "It ought to hold up the heaviest wagons that ever rolled."

"All right," said Clay, "I want two of your men to ride captured horses and march these prisoners off toward Lynchburg. The prisoners walk, though. We'll keep the rest of the horses here."

Quickly the prisoners were lined up for the journey. "Not you, Colonel Tryon," said Clay suddenly. "You'd break away somewhere and warn your friends. Stay here with me."

"As you wish," assented Tryon cordially. "I've always enjoyed your company."

"And I've always enjoyed yours." Clay watched the two mounted guardsmen escorting their captives away. "All I ask is that they keep those blue boys of yours walking until dawn. If there's an escape after that, nobody can get back in time to give any damaging information."

Tryon lighted a cigar. "In other words," he ventured, "your army's going to try to smash through here at sunrise."

Bob Dulin glanced up sharply from beside Chadwick. Jim Sloan too stared at Tryon, who had guessed so well.

"I didn't say that," said Clay carelessly. "Where's

that sergeant? Can your men ride, Sergeant? Because we have half a dozen horses here, and we can act as a mounted detail when things begin to happen."

"When the Union army comes and scoops you in," elaborated Tryon genially.

"When the Union army comes it'll be retreating too fast to scoop in anybody," said Clay. "Sergeant, we'll cross and wait on both sides of the road by the bridge. No Yankee must destroy it. As Colonel Tryon seems to know so well, Robert E. Lee himself will come across here, riding his big gray horse Traveller. It's our job to see the bridge isn't wrecked."

"Not one man of your army will ever get this far," Tryon teased.

"Wrong. Three of us are here already, not counting the home guards."

"Touché!" laughed Tryon. "I wonder if your friend Dulin made enough coffee for us all to have some. It'll help pass the time."

Together they returned to the fireside. Bob was supporting Chadwick's head on his arm, and held a steaming cup to Chadwick's lips. Chadwick drank and smiled, and Bob smiled back.

"It seems to me," said Tryon, "that I heard Dulin say once that it was his ambition to kill a hundred Federals. I was a prisoner that time, and glad he wasn't after me."

"They killed my brothers," said Bob, "but all their blood won't bring my brothers back. I've taken time to realize that. Just now my ambition's to see this poor fellow back on his feet."

"Spoken like a man and a soldier," applauded Tryon.

He took the coffeepot from the coals and poured cupfuls for himself, Jim, and Clay.

Clay told the sergeant to mount his men and watch to the east from the far side of the bridge. He and Jim sat on the ground with Tryon, and Bob found another blanket to wrap around the suffering Chadwick. They all drank coffee, and Tryon entertained them with stories of his adventures before the war.

They were good stories, for Tryon had helped lay out railroads beyond the Mississippi, had journeyed to California with settlers in a covered wagon train, and had studied at a German university. He had heard Abraham Lincoln debate with Stephen A. Douglas, had known Sam Houston as governor of Texas and Jeb Stuart as a cavalry lieutenant on the Kansas plains.

"The west is a wonderful country of opportunity," he summed up his tale. "Remember what Horace Greeley said?"

"I remember," spoke up Jim. "Go west, young man. Well, the whole Army of Northern Virginia will be passing this way soon, on its way west. What time is it?"

Tryon pulled out a gold watch and consulted it by the light of the fire.

"Four o'clock, and past," he informed them. "Your friends will attack at dawn, I suppose."

Chadwick lay silent, and Bob Dulin was distressed

for a moment, then relieved as he saw the man he had wounded was asleep. He besought the others to keep quiet, and they sat or lounged without talk. At last the skies in the east grew gray.

Then, suddenly, a rolling burst of gunfire sounded from the direction of the coming dawn, and another. Clay jumped up and sprinted across the bridge.

In the distance were belts of woods, visible now that the light had come, but he could not see what was happening beyond them. The firing grew louder and more incessant, and the boom of cannon tore through the rattle of muskets.

Tryon hurried to Clay's elbow. "That sounds like a full-dress, big-name military action," he said excitedly.

"Right," said Clay. "But we're out of it for now. Let's go back and see what's for breakfast."

The home guards had an ample provision, slices of cold beef between split biscuits. Everyone ate but Chadwick. Bob Dulin and the doctor's son gave him more coffee, and examined his wound. It did not seem to be bleeding, and Chadwick thanked his attendants for their care. The sun rose, and still the firing continued beyond the trees to the east.

"This food reminds me of a picnic back home," commented Jim, biting into another beef sandwich.

"With pretty music and everything," added Clay above the noise of the unseen guns.

Often before, Clay had eaten to the sound of battle, and had learned not to flinch as he ate. But the fight yonder was at Appomattox Court House, or near it. What might be happening to Lark? He dared not try to guess. He looked at the spring leaves on the trees around him, looked up at the sky. He tried to push the din of explosions and volleys out of his mind.

"You're worried," said Tryon beside him.

"Not about the outcome of this battle."

"But you're worried about something." Tryon regarded him searchingly. "I'm your friend, Clay. What's troubling you?"

Clay drew a deep breath. "It's about Miss Lark Winstead. She's yonder in that little town."

"I'm sorry to hear it," said Tryon.

They said no more, because there was nothing to say. They waited. The noise of the fight did not abate. Time wore on and on. It was the middle of the morning. No sign of troops coming from the east. The morning moved toward noon. Then, suddenly—

There was silence, utter and deadening silence.

Tryon and Clay looked at each other. They looked at the home guards, at the prone Chadwick in his swaddling of blankets, at Bob Dulin and the doctor's son sitting beside him.

"What's happening?" asked Jim Sloan, mystified.

Clay shook his head. "It sounds to me as if nothing's happening. As if suddenly everything stopped happening."

They could hear the cheeping of birds, the rustling of wind among the spring leaves. They waited, and the silence hung about them.

"What shall we do?" asked the sergeant, still turning to Clay as his commander.

"I can't tell you that until we know what's going on there," and Clay nodded toward the thickets that masked happenings to the east of them.

"And how can we find that out?" wondered Jim.

"I'll go and see."

Clay said those words suddenly, without waiting to ponder over the decision. He walked toward Cherokee, tied with other horses to a young oak.

"Jim," he said, "I'm going to leave you in charge here. You guardsmen, this is Jim Sloan. He's a veteran Iron Scout. Do what he tells you while I'm gone."

"Are you going alone?" asked Tryon.

"No, I'm not," replied Clay, again making up his mind on the instant. "You come with me."

Tryon looked his amazement.

"I mean that," said Clay seriously. "For the moment you can forget that you're a prisoner. We'll ride out there together and find out what stopped all the shooting."

"If my side is holding the road—" began Tryon.

"If your side's holding the road, I'll probably land right among your soldiers," Clay finished the sentence for him. "With you beside me, I won't get shot down without questions."

"That's right," said Tryon, and smiled. "And if we run into your side instead, you'll save me."

He mounted his own horse. Together he and Clay

rode eastward toward the timber. Neither of them spoke.

As they rode through the trees and into the open beyond, they were among Federals. Men in blue uniforms sat in relaxed groups, or leaned on their rifles. Farther along, larger bodies of Federal soldiers could be seen. A horseman came toward them, and when he saw Tryon he saluted.

"Sir, who is this Rebel you have with you?" he inquired. He was a young lieutenant.

"A friend of mine," said Tryon. "A friend of years' standing."

"But what's he doing over here with us? The Rebels aren't supposed to leave their position."

"What are you talking about?" demanded Tryon. "What's going on here? I haven't been with the army all night."

"Oh, don't you know, sir? There's been a white flag passed."

"White flag!" echoed Clay.

"That's right," said the lieutenant. "General Grant's just left to go into that little town out there."

"Appomattox Court House," Tryon told him the name.

"Yes, sir. General Grant's at a house belonging to somebody named McLean, we hear. He and General Lee are arranging the surrender of the Rebel army."

≫ 17 ≪
The Dawn of Peace

Clay sat stolidly on Cherokee without stirring hand or foot. He felt like a man turned into wood, stiff and lifeless and mindless. Somebody touched his shoulder. It was Tryon.

"Clay," said Tryon gently, "I ought to be glad, but somehow I feel sorry."

"Thanks," mumbled Clay.

"It's all over," went on Tryon, his voice still hushed.

"Yes, I'm thankful for that, too."

Tryon addressed the lieutenant: "I want you to escort this man through our lines and see that he gets back to his own side. Clay, I think I'll head for the bridge again. I'll find a surgeon to look after Chadwick, and maybe I'll see you later."

He rode off quickly, as though to leave Clay to his own thoughts. After a moment Clay, too, rode away eastward with the lieutenant.

"How did it all happen?" asked Clay.

"Well, it was a mighty stiff little tussle we had," was

the reply. "For a while your boys had ours sort of on the run, but then reinforcements got here from our other camps to the south. And I guess your General Lee just stopped trying to get away from us."

Clay said nothing.

"I don't know what kept you going this long," said the lieutenant.

"I don't, either," said Clay.

They were silent there. They did not even say good-by when the Federal had seen Clay through the front line of massed, silent blue infantry. Alone, Clay rode to where his own comrades waited on the slope he had left the night before. Beyond at his right he saw the houses of Appomattox Court House. One of them would be the house of Wilmer McLean, where Lark Winstead waited—where Robert E. Lee was surrendering to Ulysses S. Grant.

And silence was everywhere, silence of gun and of voice and of movement.

Clay dismounted in the midst of the survivors of the Second Corps. They had squatted down by regiments; and the regiments for the most part were smaller than companies had been at the war's beginning. After a while, an hour or more later, Jim Sloan came riding from the direction of the Federal lines. He dropped off his horse beside Clay.

"Bob Dulin's staying with that Yank he wounded," reported Jim. "There's a surgeon there, and he says the wound won't be fatal, but Bob won't leave until he's sure. He told that fellow—Chadwick—that all his brothers had been killed, and Chadwick says he'll be Bob's brother. What do you think of that?"

After a while they led their horses to find the other couriers. Over small fires their comrades were cooking their noonday meal.

"Those Yanks divided their rations with us," Sergeant Drumm greeted them. "Look, here's some bacon, a whole pound for each of you. And all this hardtack. And real coffee, and sugar to go with it."

It was noon, and they fried slices of bacon, then toasted the hardtack and dipped it in the fat. They ate heartily but not happily. The couriers around them were equally gloomy and silent. Not until they had finished eating did they begin to talk. And the talk was not about war, but about peace.

"I've been studying to be a teacher," said Drumm. "I hope I can pick up my studies where I left off to be a soldier."

"Me, I was a clerk in a store," chimed in another. "If the store's still there when I get back, maybe my job will be there, too. What about you, Buckner?"

"I'll be a farmer," said Clay. "My father will be glad to see me home in time to help him with the spring plowing."

That night they slept, wearily and dreamlessly. The next day the regiments assembled while adjutants read aloud a written order from General Lee. Gordon himself read it to his staff:

"After four years of arduous service, marked by un-

surpassed courage and fortitude, the Army of Northern
Virginia has been compelled to yield to overwhelming
numbers and resources. . . ."

When he had done, Gordon passed out printed slips
of paper, the blanks filled in with names written in ink.
Clay looked at his:

> The bearer, *Private Clay Buckner, hdq. 2nd
> Corps,* being a paroled prisoner of the Army of
> Northern Virginia, may go to his home and there
> remain undisturbed.

More food arrived from Union commissaries. Clay
gazed away toward the little town, wondering about
Lark Winstead at the home of the McLeans; but Gordon had ordered the troops of his corps to remain in
their camps until further notice. Clay did stroll near
some cavalry lines, however, and someone told him that
Bob Dulin had rejoined, happy because the wounded
Chadwick had been pronounced definitely out of danger.

The next day wore away, and the next. Then on
April 12 commands came to muster regiments, brigades, and divisions. The Second Corps would lead the
last march of the Army of Northern Virginia, to lay
down its arms.

Clay and Jim and the other couriers formed in
column of fours, on horseback, behind Gordon and the
officers of the staff. Glancing to the rear, Clay saw the
infantry drawn up in column, with torn, powder-

stained flags flying overhead. So small had the regiments become that the flags were close together, almost like a garden of red and blue flowers, thought Clay.

"Shoulder arms!" rang out an order, and other voices in units to the rear repeated it. Then, from Gordon, "Forward—march!"

They tramped as though on parade, out of their camp and down the slope and along the road toward a field where a silent, close-drawn blue line stood—a Federal brigade drawn up with its muskets at the order. Forward walked the horses of Gordon's staff, and watching them at the flank of the Federal formation, a mounted general sat his black steed. Suddenly the general's voice rose, loud and clear:

"Present—arms!"

With a single concerted snap the Northern muskets came to the present, as in a salute of honor. Clay, riding behind, saw Gordon's straight back draw straighter. Gordon's gleaming saber rose in salute, then dropped its point to his stirrup. On past the silent soldiers in blue, each with musket perpendicular in front of his chest and face, passed Gordon, passed the staff officers, passed Clay and his companions. Glancing sidelong, Clay thought he saw one or two bronzed Northern faces twitch as though in emotion. No sound, though, save the trampling of hoofs, and the rhythmic marching of feet.

On they moved, and on, until Gordon had passed the extreme flank of the watching line of Federals. Then came his bugle-like order to halt, and the infantry of the Second Corps stopped. Gordon led his mounted party to the side and away.

The officers of the regiments were taking over:

"Right—face!"

Then, "Stack—arms!"

The men built their muskets into little pyramids. Upon these were laid the battle-torn flags. Drumm collected the weapons of the couriers. Clay gave up his own revolver and the one he had taken from Tryon.

Back to camp trudged the Second Corps. Gordon checked his horse, and men thronged around him as he sat in the saddle. Clay saw his general's lined cheeks gleaming with tears.

"Soldiers!" Gordon called out in a choked voice. "No mathematician can compute the odds against which you have fought. . . ."

The veterans wept as they listened. Clay felt his own throat tighten, felt his own eyes fill up. This was the end of the war, the end of the Confederacy, the end of everything—

"No," he corrected himself under his breath, "not the end of everything."

"It's your duty as patriots to remain and work for your homes and your people," Gordon was finishing. "Enter cheerfully and hopefully upon the tasks you must perform. Obey the laws. Give the same loyal support to the Union government that you have given to the Confederacy. You have been brave, and your opponents have been brave. Join hands with them in peace and friendship."

Up went Gordon's gloved hand. "That is all. We can go home now."

Clay shook hands with all his comrades, and promised to write to Jim Sloan as soon as he got back to Northampton County. Then he urged Cherokee toward the town and along the little main street. Union soldiers moved along the walks and stood at the corners. One or two waved to him in friendly fashion. Up ahead of Clay an officer in blue ambled along on his horse, and Clay caught up with him.

"Excuse me, sir," he said, "do you know where the Wilmer McLean house is?"

"I'm going there myself," was the reply, and a side-whiskered face turned. "Hello, Clay Buckner."

"Colonel Tryon!"

Clay's gray-sleeved arm swung across, and Tryon's blue-sleeved arm rose to meet it. Joyfully they shook hands.

"You told me that Miss Lark Winstead was at Mc-Lean's," said Tryon. "I was going to offer her whatever assistance I could. Come on, Clay, we'll greet her together."

They trotted along the street and dismounted before a red brick house. They knocked at the door and were met by Major Wilmer McLean himself. A moment later Lark had rushed from the rear of the house, and was hugging Clay in a breathless storm of laughter and happy tears.

"You're all right!" she kept crying. "You're safe!"

"He looks safe now, I think," observed Tryon to McLean.

"Lark," said Clay, "this is Colonel Tryon of General Grant's staff, an old friend of mine. You met him once yourself, long ago."

"Early in the war, Miss Winstead," contributed Tryon. "I was in civilian clothes then, making observations. Oh, well, let's just say I was spying."

"The point is, I've kept running into him all through the war," pursued Clay. "We've spied on each other, captured each other, fought each other—"

"But we've never ceased to be friends," interrupted Tryon. "Speaking for myself, at least. And we're both glad the fighting's over."

He bowed low to Lark, as graceful and cordial as though asking her for the next dance at a grand ball.

"I've heard much about Colonel Tryon, from you and the other Iron Scouts," said Lark to Clay. "I think they liked and respected him more than any other Yankee."

"I like and respect another," Clay told her. "General Grant. Did you hear that he gave rations to our army, and said that the men might keep their horses?"

"That's true," seconded Tryon. "I know at least twenty of our officers who are mourning because they haven't a chance to claim Cherokee from Clay."

They moved into a parlor. It was almost stripped of furniture.

"This is where General Lee accepted General

Grant's terms," McLean said. "Union officers have been buying our chairs and tables for souvenirs. Wait, I'll bring you something to sit on."

Lark and Clay and Tryon smiled at each other. Lark looked tired and tense, and she wore her dark dress with the white cuffs and collar. It was patched and mended here and there. But her smile was bright.

"And now what must you do?" she asked Clay.

"I can go home," said Clay. "I have my parole here in my pocket. I came to see what could be done for you."

"I want to go home, too," she said eagerly. "I mean, back with you to Northampton County, where Grandmother and my Aunt Celie and your folks are all together in one house."

"There's a horse that Lark can have," said McLean, returning. "All that has kept her here as long as this is that I've been afraid to let her start that long ride alone. It's nearly a hundred miles."

"She won't be alone now," spoke up Tryon. "Clay Buckner is as fine an escort as a lady would want. Are you armed, Clay?"

"No, sir, I gave up my revolvers today."

"Well, take this."

From his holster Tryon drew a fine revolver. "You took this from me back there at that bridge on the way to Lynchburg; I reclaimed it from the surrendered arms; and now you can have it as a little reminder of me."

Thankfully Clay accepted the weapon. "I'm in your debt," he said.

"And I'll write to you in Northampton County when I have an address to give you," went on Tryon. "Peace is going to bring lots of problems. If you need help, and if there is anything that I can do for you, call on me."

Clay grasped Tryon's hands in his. "Thank you!" he cried. "I don't know what else to say."

"What else can anybody say?" asked Lark.

Tryon smiled from one to the other.

"Now, excuse me," he said. "I'm going to hurry back to our headquarters. If you're going to take that long ride, you'll need provisions. People along the way will give you lodging, but after all this fighting and foraging over the country there won't be much to eat. So I'll be right back with supplies."

He smiled again, bowed quickly, and walked out of the room.

Clay and Lark looked at each other.

"Today's Wednesday," said Lark. "If we start now, we ought to be with our folks by next Sunday. That's Easter."